Skizzer

Skizzer

A Novel

A. J. KIESLING

Published by Revell
a division of Baker Publishing Group
P.O. Box 6287, Grand Rapids, MI 49516-6287
www.revellbooks.com

Printed in the United States of America

Library of Congress Cataloging-in-Publication Data
Kiesling, Angela.
Skizzer : a novel / A.J. Kiesling.
p. cm.
ISBN 978-0-8007-3140-3 (pbk.)
1. Missing persons—Fiction. 2. Sisters—Fiction. 3. Family—Fiction. I. Title.
PS3611.I448S58 2008
813′.6—dc22 2007038767

For Kate and Emily

1

Gideon, North Carolina
June 2001

The events of the summer that changed our lives might never have come together as they did if I had not stopped for fast food before reaching my aunt's house near Raleigh. In a sense, that one simple decision affected all our lives—the way a fallen log in a river diverts water into a tributary, slowly over time. You don't notice the difference at first. Then you wake up one day and realize that where you are is not where you meant to be going, that the person you've become is not who you thought you'd be. And that deductive reasoning—working backward in time, over all the details and events—leads you squarely to that one moment that turned out to be the genesis of change.

By the time I crossed the Virginia–North Carolina border the rain had spent itself to little more than a drizzle. The wind lashed at my windshield, and in spite of the muggy air outside I felt a chill run down my spine. I clung to the wheel, nearly hypnotized by the rhythmic slapping of the wipers, and cursed my foolish fear of flying. At the turnoff for Gideon, I hesitated only a second when the hamburger sign emerged from behind a clump of kudzu. I swerved my car onto the exit ramp and made my way down Route 21 to the restaurant, gazing at the familiar landscape that was little changed even after my long absence. As I ate my cheeseburger an idea took shape in my mind, and I realized with sudden clarity that I had to follow it. Pure instinct urged me to detour seven miles out of my way to the ragged landscape of the old Radcliffe place, where we used to play as children.

Something about the old house pulled at me. Not just the way its blackened window spaces stared back like empty eye sockets. Not even the memories tied so inextricably to this place. If my sister Becca had left any clue as to her whereabouts—anything that could explain her sudden disappearance a week ago—it would be here. I knew it. I felt it in my bones. That same sort of gut *knowing* had led me to make the twelve-hour drive from Florida to visit Aunt Jess, and North Carolina, to begin with. For here is where Becca's and my roots lay deep and gnarled as those of the giant sycamore tree that stood outside our bedroom window when we were girls.

The long-abandoned house was nestled in a cradle of Southern pines at the point where the woods met the open meadow—now a thinning field cut in two by the access road that led to our old neighborhood's entrance. Across the street stood the family plot, a small graveyard caged by a rusted wrought-iron fence. A dozen faded tombstones slanted out from the weeds that choked the ground, reminding trespassers that other people once laid claim to this land. Picking my way through the sodden undergrowth, I walked around to the back of the house. How long had it been since Becca and I played here, the waving goldenrod transforming into bulrushes along the Nile, where we always found a hapless baby doll—conveniently planted there by one or the other of us before the game began?

Reaching the back door, I placed my toes against the stone slab that served as a step and started counting, taking one step backward with each count until I reached thirteen. I noticed a patch of earth that looked recently turned. Grabbing a brick fragment from the ground, I dug at the wet soil until my fingers hurt. About six inches down, the brick struck metal.

I clawed a little moat around the perimeter of a small metal box and lifted it out. Besides a coating of rust, the faded pink box looked just as I remembered it. What was it Becca had told me that steamy Sunday afternoon in 1977, two months after we discovered the cottage in the woods? I scrounged in my memory for the strange rhyming words, but they wouldn't come. Something about dreams and schemes, breath and death—creepy words for two young girls, it occurred to me now. Her amber brown eyes had fixed me with that odd penetrating look they got whenever she was on to one of her otherworldly tangents. On this particular day, Baby Moses—who bore a striking resemblance to my old Betty Burp Me doll and now sported a boyish bowl cut—had been tossed aside after a half hour of play, and Becca produced a small pink metal box with a keyhole shaped like a daisy. I recognized it as her Christmas gift from Aunt Jess that year. Not too special at the time—just one of many presents she and I had opened Christmas morning. But now, as she produced a gold key from her pocket and poised it ceremoniously above the box, Aunt Jess's gift seemed imbued with mysterious significance.

Again, those amber eyes stared at me solemnly.

"What, Becca? You're creeping me out," I said, scratching absently at a new mosquito bite.

"If I tell you, you've got to swear to keep it a secret till your dying day," my melodramatic sister intoned. She paused and looked past my shoulder at something. The fading sunlight cast a pinkish glow around her face. "Claire, have you ever thought how this very moment in time will never come again? Like, if you could catch a little piece of it and cup it in your hand like a firefly, you could take it with you and peek inside at the light every once in a while?"

"Yeah, I guess so," I lied. Did I ever think like that? For my sister's sake, I wanted to believe so.

"Well," she continued, "I definitely do. Now, look in here."

She opened the lid of the pink box, and I was allowed

to gaze on its treasures for the first time. Among an assortment of trinkets, I saw something that actually looked expensive—a gold pendant in the shape of a crescent moon, encrusted with a tiny ruby as the man in the moon's eye. It was an odd piece of jewelry and odder still because it was in my sister's possession. It looked very old.

"Hey, where'd you get this?" I plucked the moon off its bed of trinkets and turned away to examine it in the pink light. "Does Mama know you have it?"

Becca shook her head silently, but she wouldn't look at me. "It's just something I found in the woods the other day."

My sister was not the best liar in the world, but she was about the most determined person I ever knew. If she didn't want to tell you something, there was no getting it out of her.

"Becca, this looks expensive. What if the owner's looking for it? I think we ought to show Mama."

"No!" she shouted, snatching the pendant out of my hand before my reflexes could curl it into a fist. "Do you want to hear the rest of what I've got to say or don't you?"

I told her I did. My sister always had the upper hand.

"There are things only a sister should know—sister secrets," she continued, her wide eyes framed by wisps of blonde hair. "We can share our sister secrets here in this little box. The gold moon will make it special."

I wondered where she was going with this; I didn't have to wait long. Holding the box close to her chest, Becca marked off a spot in the ground, stooped down, and dug a hole there. As we covered the pink box with dirt, she made me swear a solemn oath never to tell another living soul about it. She was so dead serious about the whole thing she made me swear on our cat Thunder's grave, and I have to admit that's a promise we both kept. In fact, neither one of us bothered much with the box after a few more years. The move to Florida put it out of our minds altogether, and not long after that we discovered boys, our first pimples, and the dozens of other diversions that draw a girl across the chasm into young womanhood.

A passing car honked, sending a flock of blackbirds fluttering out of the pine boughs overhead. Spooked, I dropped the rusty metal box. I muttered a mild expletive as I picked the box back up and pried the lid open, the brass hinges creaking in protest. Unbelievably, my highway hunch paid off. There inside the box, amid a jumble of baubles and other mementos, lay a beige envelope inscribed with a familiar sloping hand. Written on it was the single word *Skizzer*, Becca's baby word for sister—the name she had called me when we were toddlers, our mother said. The gold crescent moon, of course, was gone.

Shoving the box under my arm, I started back toward the car to read the envelope's contents out of the drizzle, which had settled into the kind of misty, hovering condensation that always wreaked havoc on my hair. I tore the envelope open; the letter inside was cryptic, true to form for Becca:

I knew you'd think to look here eventually, even though it's been a long time. Something both terrible and wonderful has happened. I can't explain now. Please don't look for me, and tell Rainey not to worry . . . I'm safe. I'll call when I'm ready. Just need some time to myself right now.

Love always, Becca

Tell Rainey not to worry? My brother-in-law was half out of his mind with panic. His frenzied phone call late on the night she had disappeared still rang clear in my head: "Claire, she's gone," his voice brusque.

"Who's gone, Rainey?" I asked, though a sudden knot in my stomach forewarned me.

"Becca. She packed her things and left. The last thing she told me was that she was going to get her hair done. That was late this afternoon while I was still at work. I thought it was unusual she was calling to tell me *that*.

When I got home from work there was a note on the kitchen table. 'Sweetheart, I need a little time away . . . I'll explain why later. Please don't worry about me.'" Rainey took a deep ragged breath, and I could hear the ice tinkling in a glass as he swirled it around and around in agitation. I'd seen him do that many times when he was under pressure.

My sister's cool, enigmatic words angered me. She had no right to go flying off with barely a word to anybody. But on the heels of this thought quickly came another. Though she had always been eccentric, Becca had a long history now of steady, dependable living. It wasn't like her to do something flighty and irresponsible. And she had a knee-jerk instinct for carpe diem. Seizing the day. Seizing the moment. If something "terrible and wonderful" had happened, I could only hope it turned out to be important enough to warrant the pain she was inflicting on Rainey.

I speed-dialed Rainey's number from my cell and waited for his tired voice to pick up on the other end of the line. My news was just the sort of dangling carrot of hope he needed right now.

2

Kellerby, England
June 1981

For all Becca's melodrama, I was the one who'd led a life worthy of any good book heroine. Full of stops and starts, disappointments, angst, and unrequited love. Then, after a fitful beginning, modest success at last, if you could call my newly acquired status as an author success. She, on the other hand, had married her high school sweetheart, a shy, handsome guy with the unlikely name of Rainald Garrett who, upon his first glimpse of Rebecca Ruth Trowling in the school cafeteria line, secretly vowed he would marry her someday. He provided her with a nice home in the shady, upscale section of a central Florida hamlet with brick-lined streets and a century-old downtown district.

In a way, Becca had always been spoiled, I suddenly realized. Never had to scratch and claw for a living the way I did. Always the preferred "baby daughter" when we were growing up, or at least that's how I remembered it. Though only fifteen months younger than me, Becca had a take-control presence that belied her faraway gazes and high-blown imagination. As her adoring older sister, I coddled her and followed her around like she was the pied piper when we were little—allowing her to drag me into situations I never would have ventured into on my own.

I think the first time I truly recognized this beguiling force at work in my sister occurred the year we turned thirteen and fourteen, respectively. It was also our last summer before leaving North Carolina for good to take up residence in Florida, where Mama had gotten a lucrative job. Aunt Jess, the only living relative on my mother's side, decided that summer to take Becca and me along with her on a "trip abroad," most likely to give us a much-needed cultural education. "Surely you can't object to *that*, Constance," my aunt had said, framing the words as a declaration rather than an appeal for permission. She never lost an opportunity to remind Mama she had married down in life, disappointing her. As if to prove her right, our father had abandoned us all when Becca and I were toddlers—and then Mama herself died in a car accident three blocks from home when we were away at college. Mama never said a word back after Aunt Jess's verbal jab, merely nodded and kept mashing a bowl of potatoes for supper.

In retrospect, I think it was that long, turbulent flight over the Atlantic that gave me the willies about air travel.

I kept my nose in a book nearly the whole time, unable to sleep for fear I'd wake up bobbing in the ocean, the plane's wreckage floating about me. When we finally touched down at Heathrow, I whispered the most earnest prayer of my life.

"Claire!" My aunt's voice snapped me out of my sleep-deprived trance. "Grab your suitcase. We've landed." Then, with a big, expansive smile that showed her yellowing dentures, "Welcome to England, girls. I'm sure you'll never forget this trip."

Indeed.

Becca rolled her eyes at me behind Aunt Jess's back and made a bow-and-arrow gesture aimed at her rear. I burst into giggles as I followed my sister up the narrow aisle that led to the plane's exit.

We toured London in style, whisked around in sleek black cabs that looked as if they belonged to a much earlier decade. Aunt Jess bustled us in and out of museums, forced us to eat steak and kidney pie, posed us in front of the Buckingham Palace guards, and generally commandeered the whole trip.

"When are we going to have some fun?" I whispered to Becca in the backseat of yet another cab as we bumped along a treacherously narrow road lined with tall hedgerows, far away from London. My sister gave an exaggerated shrug and turned to gaze at the hedgerow, catching glimpses of sheep-dotted meadows through gaps in the bushes. After a few minutes of silence, she suddenly leaned over and whispered in my ear.

"Aunt Jess says our next stop is a haunted rectory. They've turned it into an inn. Maybe we'll get to see a real ghost!" Her eyes shone with excitement, and I caught her infectious spirit for this unexpected bonus. I had inquired about the night's lodging earlier that day myself while Aunt Jess and I waited to make a transatlantic phone call at one of London's famous red phone booths. She told me the Rectory belonged to a distant relation, a Mrs. Lockwood, whom Aunt Jess had unearthed through genealogy research at the library. Her knowledge of the family history reached back far enough in the States, but here was a real prize in her eyes—a widowed relation who lived in the same English town of Kellerby that some of our ancestors hailed from. She hadn't mentioned anything about the place being haunted, but I'd read in several travel pamphlets about England's long history of haunts and of course its Druidic past.

After another half hour of bumping along, the Rectory sprang into view behind a clump of wild roses, one half of its façade swallowed by ivy. The house looked unassuming at first glance, and I never imagined the significance it would play in my life, not just over the next few days but years later as well. A sign with the single word "Accommodations" squeaked on its hinges as it swung from a post planted by the roadside. Someone had built the white, two-story Tudor house close to the rural route, and as the cab turned into the circular gravel drive, its tires crunching and spitting, I saw that the grounds behind the house contained a walled garden.

While Aunt Jess paid the cabby—making it clear she expected him to carry our luggage inside ("Young man, this way! Follow me")—we hurtled out of the cab to start exploring. Becca grabbed my hand and pulled me around the side of the rectory, where a dirt road disappeared over a small rise. A crop of green hills lay on the horizon.

"Thank goodness we're finally out of that cab." My sister sighed noisily. "I was starting to think my legs would never unkink. Hey, Claire, what's that?"

I turned to look in the direction of her gaze and saw a stone structure with a spire poking through the treetops. "Just some old church."

Instead of replying, Becca picked up her pace, her bright blue Keds kicking up a small cloud of dust behind her. I matched my stride to hers, my heart thumping at the prospect of what we might find in the churchyard. But our expedition would have to wait.

"Rebecca, Claire! Come help me with these suitcases," Aunt Jess bellowed, her gray cropped head looking strangely small from the short distance we'd walked down the road. "That scoundrel of a cab driver refused me."

Aunt Jess, of course, chose the bedroom facing the walled garden, but Becca and I were given a truly wonderful room. Situated upstairs, with a large picture window overlooking the wild roses in that tiny front yard, it had old-fashioned sloping ceilings with exposed beams and a giant four-poster bed. Best of all, someone had cut an opening through a sidewall that led to a small alcove. Inside the miniature room stood a single bed and a child-sized bureau. It might have belonged to a girl heroine in one of the books I'd read, and I knew instantly we were going to fight over it.

"Wow," Becca breathed over my shoulder as she peeked inside. "I claim it."

"Oh no you don't. This one's mine." I turned and planted my hands on my hips the way Mama did whenever she meant business. "I saw it first."

"Yes, but it's small like me." Becca pirouetted as if to prove she were the more deserving recipient of the secret chamber. I held my ground.

"Becca, you always get your way. For once, I'm going to get mine." I looked my sister in the eye, sure she would back down. Instead, she compromised.

"Okay, how 'bout this? You take the first night and then we'll switch off. Aunt Jess says we might stay here for a few days. She also said we had to unpack before exploring the grounds, but I don't think Her Highness will really bother to check. Why don't we poke around in here first—old houses are always full of nooks and crannies; I think I saw a staircase leading to a third floor even—and then we can go see that church down the road."

"Good plan," I agreed, putting away a few of my things despite Becca's suggestion. I placed my travel pillow on the small bed inside the alcove to stake my claim to it for that first night. Neither of us said what was really on our minds—that whoever slept in the big four-poster bed, sprawling out there in the wide open expanse of the main bedroom, would also be wide open to ethereal nighttime visitors. The nook provided a security blanket by its very closeness. Yet we *had* looked forward to the thrill of staying in a real haunted house.

At dinner that night, Mrs. Lockwood presided over the dining table like a queen. She seemed delighted to have distant relations for guests. Apparently reserved by nature, she must have worked to develop the quiet sociability one expected from the proprietor of an English lodging establishment. Our silverware tinkled, filling the emptiness whenever the conversation lulled between the two women. Becca and I sat silent, waiting for the adults to navigate the evening's events.

"As I was saying, Rev. Croker was the last full-time vicar to serve this parish, and that was nearly twenty years ago." Mrs. Lockwood twinkled her eyes at us as if this gem of information would be the highlight of our trip. "It's too bad about his wife, though. She died in childbirth, poor thing, and he never got over it."

Becca and I exchanged meaningful glances.

"He tried to continue ministering, but his heart was not in it. After a few years he just left one day and never came back. No one's heard from him since. The parish board tried out a few interim rectors, but nobody seemed fit for the job. I guess it's difficult to fill a beloved vicar's shoes. And I must confess, his disappearance caused quite a tempest in this little town."

"Are you sure he didn't run off with some woman?" Aunt Jess blurted. "Men do that sort of thing all the time." She pinned the proprietress with a knowing stare. You could have heard a pin drop on Mrs. Lockwood's polished oak floors. The innkeeper cleared her throat and reached for her glass of red wine. "Dear me, no. If that had been the case, I'm sure the whole town would have known. No, Rev. Croker had too fine a nature for that sort of thing." Her eyes glistened with some long-held remembrance, and I wondered what tidbit of local lore she would offer up next.

"Why didn't any of the other priests work out?" Aunt Jess wanted to know. "Did the ghost of the vicar's wife torment *their* wives, or was it the good reverends themselves who couldn't bear up under the presence of a dead woman hanging around the place?"

Mrs. Lockwood smiled demurely and took a sip of her wine. "Miss Trowling, I'm sure I don't know what you're talking about. Surely you don't listen to rumors."

Becca jabbed me under the table with her elbow.

"In my experience, rumors often contain more truth than lies," Aunt Jess continued. "But I'm a no-nonsense person when it comes to such things as ghosts. If spirits do indeed walk these halls, as someone informed me at the tourism office, then we'll just brace ourselves for a spine-tingling adventure, won't we, girls?" She trained her bright eyes on Becca and me. "No trip to England would be complete without encountering a ghost. This is the land of the Druids, after all."

By now Becca's amber eyes were as round as saucers, but she cast a delighted grin my way. Mrs. Lockwood scraped her chair back loudly from the table and excused herself, claiming some errand in the kitchen. Aunt Jess wore a satisfied expression that grated on me.

I waited a few seconds and then ventured a question. "Why would death from childbirth cause someone to be a ghost? I mean, it's not like that wasn't fairly common in the past."

Becca's fork clattered on her plate. "I read this story once where this man fell in love with this lady and she got really sick and died, and he actually *wanted* to see her ghost—he begged her to come back and haunt him. And this other person came to stay there years later and saw the lady ghost at his bedroom window, and it scared the living daylights out of him, so he ran and told the man who lived there. The man went up to the window and cried out for her to come back. It was creepy—I loved it."

"This isn't *Wuthering Heights*," I said, rolling my eyes at Becca. "Aunt Jess, do you know which room she died in, the preacher's wife, I mean?"

"I would imagine the main bedroom, the room where you and your sister are staying tonight."

I don't have to tell you that neither Becca nor I slept a wink that night. She stayed up late with me, sitting on the edge of the small bed in the alcove and casting furtive glances back over her shoulder into the larger room as we talked. Once or twice we both swore we felt a sudden chill, and each time we ducked under the covers in a fit of frightful ecstasy. But no ghost materialized. No moaning or shrieking broke the still night air. Becca never did make it back to the four-poster bed, and sometime right before dawn we must have fallen into a light sleep. When my full bladder woke me, I peeked at the illuminated hands on my wristwatch and realized I'd been asleep for only an hour or so.

Daylight was gathering dimly through the curtained window, but I was still too petrified to go out into the hall by myself. Nudging Becca awake, I told her to stand guard while I stole down the hallway to the toilet.

"Right now, Claire? I'm so sleepy." Her head lolled back onto the pillow. I shook her awake again.

"Becca, I have to go! Come on, now. You're the one who was too chicken to go back to your own bed last night."

"All right, all right." She threw her stockinged feet over the side of the bed and followed me as far as the bedroom doorway. She peered after me as I crept down the hallway toward the bathroom, which lay at the far end by a door Mrs. Lockwood had told us not to open.

I glanced at the forbidden door as I passed and noticed it was slightly ajar. Curiosity temporarily stalled my bathroom mission. I took one look back at Becca's pale face shining like the moon in the eerie morning light and stuck my head around the edge of the door. While I watched, a long form lying on a bed started to move, emitting a low moan from under a white sheet. I screamed and ran back down the hallway. "In there! In there! The ghost is in there!" A door slammed open, and Aunt Jess emerged, her head wrapped in a turban. She looked as if she'd seen a ghost herself. In the instant before Becca jumped into action I saw a fierce, determined expression cross my sister's face. She bolted down the hall toward the ghost room and, standing in the doorway, made a cross with two fingers and shouted, "The power of Christ compels you! The power of Christ compels you!"

"What are you doing, kid?" a deep male voice boomed, rooting Becca to the floor. "Are you trying to wake the dead or something?" By now the young man had reached the threshold of his room, and as Becca stepped backward I saw that he was not at all the sinister spirit we had conjured in our minds.

"For the love of Betsy, what's going on out here?" Aunt Jess demanded, holding onto the banister railing for support. "Girls, are you out of your minds screaming in the middle of the night like that?"

"It's not the middle of the night anymore, Aunt Jess," I offered helpfully. "The daylight's—"

"I know what time it is. I can see the daylight as well as anyone." She turned her head back in the direction of the grizzled young man who still stood in his bedroom doorway. "May we have the pleasure of your acquaintance, sir? And I do apologize for my niece's rude awakening."

Mrs. Lockwood materialized at the top of the stairs. With a cool assessment of the situation, she turned to my aunt and then looked at Becca and me. "Ladies, let me introduce my son, Colin, just home from university—apparently in the middle of the night." The look she gave him said clearly she wished he'd had the foresight to warn her.

I got my first good look at Colin Lockwood later that day when Becca and I went out to the walled garden to escape Aunt Jess's ponderous presence. Becca and I chased butterflies while she recounted the night's adventures between fits of laughter. While Becca continued her monologue a few yards behind me, I pushed aside the leaves of a willow tree, following a butterfly I'd seen disappear behind the wispy green curtain. As I emerged on the other side my breath caught in my throat. Shielded from the rest of the garden was a small glade that looked to be transported straight from the Garden of Eden. Carpeted with thick, silky grass, the glade formed a miniature garden within a garden, and I saw that I was not the first person to fall under its spell. Our ghost from the previous night sat on his haunches, tending a small flower border that ran alongside a brook. Whoever built the garden wall years ago had cleverly designed it to allow the brook to continue undisturbed on its way, flowing beneath a small archway in the wall's base.

Colin Lockwood shook back a forelock of brown hair and looked sideways up at me. A smile lifted one corner of his mouth.

"Boo!" He laughed softly at his little joke and turned back to his gardening. My cheeks burned hotly.

"So what brings two American girls to our little haunted rectory? Mum told me you plan to stay for a few days."

"Yeah," I said, mentally kicking myself for suddenly going mute. Colin had a lean, muscular physique, and I watched his forearms twitch as he plied the earth to plant five new pots of perennials. A scar ran from his right temple midway down his cheek, but the effect only made him more alluring somehow. He looked like someone who spent a lot of time outdoors; I guessed him to be about twenty-three. Grateful Becca had not followed me into the glade, I sat down at a tentative distance and said the first thing that popped into my mind.

"So, is there really a ghost, Mr. Lockwood?"

"Hey, now, no need to be doing that. Colin's fine. Don't make me feel older than I already am." He winked at me. Death by flirtation, I thought as my center turned on its axis. "Sure, there's a real spook, but it's probably not the one you were expecting. After I finish planting these I'll take you and your sister out to the church and tell you the story. That's where it really happened, you know."

As he talked about the flowers and how he studied botany "away at university," I grew comfortable in his easygoing presence. With his focus on the plants, I was free to gaze unhindered at the man in front of me. His shoulder-length brown hair tied back in a ponytail, Colin was as mesmerizing to me as Heathcliff must have been to Isabella Linton—only not nearly so fierce. His hands seemed made for the earth. I watched fascinated as his fingers alternately patted and plucked, easing the flowers into their new home by the brook. He stood to dust off the knees of his blue jeans. "You ready?" He lifted his eyes to mine. I registered their color for the first time—dark brown—and nodded. "Why don't you go get your sister while I wash off my hands. I'll meet you two out on the road in a minute."

I ducked back under the hanging green curtain of willow tree branches and found Becca playing with Mrs. Lockwood's Yorkshire puppy, Samson, against the far wall. She was immediately game for our next adventure, and when we joined Colin on the dirt road a few minutes later she monopolized the conversation.

"This old church, St. Barnabas, dates back to the 1400s," Colin interjected as we approached the stone structure through a clearing in the trees several yards from the road. "Not too many come around anymore, but when I was a kid tourists were always stopping by to see the devil face."

"The what?" Becca and I said, almost in unison.

Colin smiled and pushed aside a low-hanging tree branch with a knobby walking stick he'd brought along from the garden shed. It made him look like a young Gandalf. "You'll see. It's that spook I was telling you about. Just so you know, it's not really the vicar's wife that gives the place its mystique, it's what happened out here, centuries ago." He pointed the stick at the church, a stout structure built of stones that had darkened to the color of flint. With the sound of Becca's rapid breathing in my ear—I knew she was loving this—I took in the scenery. An ancient graveyard flung on one side of the church bore headstones with dates all but eroded. A bell tower directly in front of us loomed out of the earth, imposing in its height. It was to that Colin now directed us, taking the steps to the bell tower two at a time.

"You see, back in 1560 another priest lost his wife here, but legend has it the good priest went mad in his grief and hanged himself from the bell tower. They didn't find his body until the faithful came to service Sunday morning three days later and saw his corpse hanging there. The townspeople declared the church as cursed, desecrated by the horrible suicide, and so they shunned it. It's said that a group of Druids was drawn to the church after that—I suppose they liked the paradox of a holy place being cursed. So it remained off-limits to anyone claiming the name of Christ for a while until a stouthearted vicar reclaimed the church building for God's use. At some point in the church's history someone carved the face of a devil in one of the stones out back. To scare away evil spirits, perhaps. Like gargoyles on a cathedral."

Becca and I were silent for several seconds as we gazed up at the crossbeam that supported the massive bell, picturing the body of a priest swinging there. I felt relieved when Colin led us back down the bell tower's stone steps to the rear exterior wall of the church. There, just as he had said, the devil's countenance glowered out at us.

Becca was the first to break the silence. "Wow. What a story." I nodded in mute agreement.

While we studied the grisly visage, Colin leaned his walking stick against the wall and retrieved a pocketknife from his jeans pocket. I watched as he cleaned the underside of each fingernail with the blade. Not saying a word, he finished the task and put the knife away.

"Did it work?" Becca asked.

Colin lifted his eyes and looked at Becca. "What's that, love?"

"The evil spirits. Did they get rid of them?"

"But of course," our handsome guide said in his cultured accent, a crooked grin on his face. "The power of Christ compelled them." He exchanged a smile with my sister, and I realized with a sudden fierceness that I had never despised Becca so much as right then.

Colin picked up his walking stick and gestured with it like a trail guide. "Come on, you two. We'd better be heading back."

I started to follow his retreating back toward the road and realized Becca wasn't behind me. Glancing over my shoulder, I saw my sister reach out, touch the stone devil face, and quietly repeat the words Colin had said—words she herself had uttered early that morning when she acted impulsively, bravely, to save me from mortal terror. As we shuffled along behind Colin, I suddenly thought to ask her aloud the question simmering in my mind all day. "Becca, where in the world did you hear such a phrase anyway?"

"What phrase?" She looked over at me, that faraway haze in her eyes again.

"That power of Christ thing." From the corner of my eye, I saw Colin glance back at us.

"Oh that." She waved her hand dismissively. "The visiting evangelist who taught our Sunday school class a few weeks ago said those words, and he seemed to put a lot of stock in them. You were home sick with the flu that Sunday, remember? But *I* sure was there, and the evangelist's words stuck with me for some reason. And they worked, don't you think?" She smiled ironically.

Though outwardly nonchalant, my sister was quiet over the next few days while we lingered on at the Rectory. I guessed she was probably savoring the story Colin had told us, the way she and I always savored a good book after turning the last page, not wanting it to end. Aunt Jess and Mrs. Lockwood had formed an unlikely friendship out of an unexpected shared affinity for small dogs. (Aunt Jess's own Chihuahua, Noodle, a terror on four legs, had been "regrettably" shunted off to the kennel for the duration of our trip.)

On the last morning of our stay the two women sat amicably in the garden trading dog stories, while Becca read a book on the four-poster bed. Feeling restless, I wandered outside and took the road down to the church. As I drew near I heard the unmistakable sound of a flute playing. I followed the sound to the bell tower, where Colin sat, one leg flung daringly over the side of the low wall, his head bent to the task of making melody.

He looked up at my approach. I saw a purple velvet drawstring bag at his feet, with several other bamboo flutes protruding from the top of it. I remembered Mrs. Lockwood saying something about his crafting the instruments for sale in his spare time. Once before I had come upon him playing a guitar in the garden at twilight, his eyes lost in the music.

Right now those eyes gazed at me steadily, and I could see them glistening with unshed tears. He didn't bother to blink them away. "The right melody is like a prayer, don't you think?" he said before he bent his head to the flute once more. "This is a prayer for you." The sound that came out gave me goose bumps it was so beautiful. I sat quietly while he finished his song and then waited for what would come next.

"You're a quiet one, Claire," Colin said as he put the flute back in the drawstring bag. It was the first time I'd ever heard him say my name. "I've watched you. You're not like everyone else; you see deeply. Don't ever lose that gift for seeing things as they really are." Though his words struck me as strange, I wanted to promise him I wouldn't—wanted to blurt that I would never forget this moment for as long as I lived—but of course nothing came out.

Colin continued. "It's funny, you know, but this old church is my favorite place to be when I need to reconnect to the spiritual—in spite of its tragic history, I mean. Old churches have that effect on me. It's as if the ancient wood of the pews, the altar, and the cross carry traces of the souls who worshipped here. I'll run my hand along the wood grain of the pews, feel the carvings made by children long ago, and sense God in this place. It's a shame St. B's has been discarded now, left to go to ruins."

I sat entranced, not wanting to interrupt his wonderful flow of words, and so he went on.

"During my first year at university, I was going through a rough time—long story, so I won't bore you with it now—and I wandered about the campus at twilight one evening. It was winter, and I nearly froze my bum off. After about an hour of this aimless rambling, I came to the university chapel and saw a glow inside. The doors were always kept unlocked, so I went inside, as much to warm up as anything. No one was around, but candles were burning on the altar. I chose a pew toward the front, wanting to be near all that glowing warmth, and I started to pray. Mind you, this was no ordinary prayer. It was the kind that wells up in the spirit without words. Suddenly a voice boomed out the opening lines of Luther's hymn: 'A mighty fortress is our God, a bulwark never failing . . .'

"I glanced around, but no one was there. In a moment of panic I wondered if my strange mood had put me in tune with a voice from the past—something otherworldly. England is famous for its spirits, you know. But common sense kicked in and I started to explore. At the third pew from the back I discovered the source of the singing—it was the sexton, lying under the pew, polishing wood no one would ever see and singing loud praises to God. That night changed me somehow. I've never looked at God the same way since."

A story like that warranted some type of response, but once again I felt myself tongue-tied in Colin's presence. Years would pass before the full weight of his story settled into my spirit, leaving its quiet residue there. The story never left me, and even today I find myself drawn to old churches because of it—seeking solace, seeking God.

"Come along," Colin said after a pause. "I'll walk you back to the house."

As we ambled up the dusty road and later said our good-byes, Becca and I waving madly from yet another sleek black cab, I cursed my misfortune at being born too late—and on the wrong side of the Atlantic.

3

Gideon, North Carolina
June 2001

I reached into my purse and felt around for Becca's letter, fearful it had somehow escaped in the thirty minutes since I left the old Radcliffe place in Gideon. Rainey had told me to phone him the minute I got a room in town. With the exception of a hot bath, I intended to make good on my promise. Though Aunt Jess lived close by, I decided she could wait till tomorrow. I hadn't talked to the old woman in years, and I wasn't ready to deal with her yet. After our move to Florida all those years ago, she stayed on in Gideon and now lived in a townhouse on the old-money side of town. Mama had encouraged her to move into an assisted-living facility—she certainly had the means to—but Aunt Jess's pride was formidable, and I doubted she needed any assistance anyway. No, for now the only person I wanted to talk to was Rainey.

My sister had managed to capture not only an honest,

hardworking man who still turned female heads when he walked into a room, but a man who adored her. While other women—myself included—lamented that "all the good ones were taken," Becca enjoyed the devoted attentions of a truly good man. My own attempt at marriage, two years after I graduated from college, failed miserably just four years later. Those wasted years with Lenny seemed a strange and distant dream to me now, like the memory of relayed events that happened to someone else. I would stare at my tall, lanky reflection in a mirror and wonder: Is it my lack of curves? Do men always prefer blondes over women with plain brown hair? Dishwater blonde, my mother used to call it, but that was fourteen years ago when it still had golden highlights. My eyes were good—my best feature, I thought—large and luminous, the color of bright seawater.

Time had marched on. All those years of searching for a face, the face of a man—my man, wherever he was—or at least something very like the face I'd encountered that summer in England when I was a girl. No one since had quite measured up to my early ideal, and he was the one I unconsciously weighed all the others against. I would glimpse a strong, sinewy forearm or see a man crouching down to retrieve something from the ground and have a sudden flashback, nearly tangible in its effect on me.

But my melancholy ran deeper than the yearning for a soul mate. The truth is I had lost touch with God over the years, or rather allowed the distance to grow between us after that early burst of expectation slowly settled into the dull drone of everyday existence. Then came disappointment and finally disillusionment—with myself, with Lenny, and with my seeming inability to be successful at anything besides writing. I had a vague sense that God was disappointed with me too. I sighed and turned on the car stereo, loud.

I left a voicemail for Aunt Jess when I got to the hotel, informing her of my whereabouts, and then drew a bath. As I sank into the steaming tub my cell phone rang. Without even looking I knew who it was. When the phone reached eight rings I realized he wasn't going to give up easily and hauled myself out of the tub.

"Hey, Rainey. You're persistent, aren't you?"

My brother-in-law was not in the mood for chitchat. "Claire, I'm flying up there—tonight. I can't bear to be down here now that I know for sure Becca passed through Gideon. I want to see that note she left you, I found something I need to show you, and I want to talk to Aunt What's-Her-Name myself." I grinned. Aunt Jess had that effect on people.

I grabbed my robe off the bathroom door and wrapped it around me, cradling the flip-phone with my chin. "Sure, Rain, do you need me to pick you up at the airport?"

"No, you stay put and get some rest. I'll take a cab to the hotel, rent a room, and then we can meet somewhere in the lobby about midnight."

"So what is it, this thing you want to show me?"

"It can wait till I get there. I figured if there's anyone

on earth who can make sense out of it, it's you. At this point, I don't even want to venture a guess without your input."

Later that night, in the dim lighting of the hotel's coffee bar, I watched Rainey's face while he read Becca's brief letter. I had read its contents to him over the phone the moment I found it at the Radcliffe place, but now he read and reread the five sentences like they were the last known missive from a war prisoner.

"Terrible and wonderful? What the heck is that supposed to mean?" Rainey pushed the letter back into its beige envelope and placed it on the table where we sat nursing decaf cappuccinos. He raked his hand through his stiff, dark curls and raised his eyes warily to mine.

"You don't think she's having an affair, do you? Be honest, Claire. Give me your gut feeling on this . . . or is there something you already know and don't want to tell me?"

I shook my head as I swallowed a mouthful of steaming liquid. "Rainey, I know Becca better than anyone in the world, and she's a rotten liar. If she were having an affair, I'd be the first to know. Besides, she's always been a one-man woman. What you have to decide now is what you want to do with this information." I pointed to the "Skizzer" letter, which, of course, contained no date. "We know she had to at least pass through North Carolina to bury this at the old house. Is there anyone around here she might have fled to for sanctuary? You know, a long-lost friend or something?"

Even as the words flew out I realized Rainey knew far less about Becca's girlfriends—new or old—than I did. They had been the sort of childless couple who became each other's entire world, content with their company of two. And though my sister had that uncanny knack for drawing people like a magnet, she also held them at arm's length. As a result, her friendships had dwindled over the years to myself and two or three women she knew from her stint as an adjunct professor at the local community college in Florida. That she might have stayed with Aunt Jess seemed a far stretch, but I didn't say so.

"Heck if I know," Rainey said, downing the last of his cappuccino and reaching into his pants pocket. "But I sure don't intend to sit around doing nothing about it. Here's that thing I wanted to show you." He pulled out a small black velvet box and handed it to me. "I've never seen her wear this in my life, and it doesn't look like the kind of jewelry she would choose anyway. What do you think?"

Inside the box lay a pendant crafted in a beguiling shape I hadn't seen for a quarter century: a gold crescent moon that stared up at me from its bed of cotton.

Involuntarily, I gasped.

"Do you recognize it? Where did she get this thing?"

"Hey, slow down, Rain. One thing at a time." I brushed the hair back from my eyes as I bent under the low ceiling lamp that hung over our table to get a better look at the strange pendant. Some inexplicable instinct told me not to spill the details of the last time I'd seen jewelry like this—and its implications for the present—but I remembered all too clearly the day, two months before Becca first showed me the pendant, when we found the cottage in the woods. It was etched on my childhood memory.

4

Gideon, North Carolina
June 1977

Rain drummed on the roof, drowning out the roar of Mama's sewing machine in the room next to Becca's and mine. Though technology had long since caught up with the late 1970s, Mama insisted on using the antique sewing machine she inherited from Aunt Jess. She drove it like a roadster, pumping the foot pedal for what seemed like hours on end until somehow, magically, the yards of fabric transformed into a dress.

Becca pressed her nose against the glass, watching rivulets of water trickle down the windowpane, and then blew a little breath of fog onto it. The steam blurred the woods that crouched at the edge of our backyard, dark and ominous in the storm.

"When will this ever end?" she groaned.

"Maybe never if you keep griping about it." I lay propped on my bed with a book open on my lap.

"Hey, I know," Becca said suddenly, an idea lighting her face. "Since we can't go outside today, why don't I call Joe and let him tell you about his surprise."

I looked up, suddenly interested.

Becca ambled toward the hallway and disappeared around the corner. Moments later, I heard her talking on the phone in the kitchen, and when she yelled for me to pick up the extension in Mama's room, I didn't hesitate. Joe Spivey was a boy in our neighborhood best known for the patch of freckles across his nose that had blended into a solid, clumpy mass. He had a penchant for blowing up insects and doing other disgusting boy things, but he was good company when he wanted to be. As I got on the phone, Joe told me in breathless tones how he'd stumbled onto something "cool" in the woods behind our house the week before. Now he couldn't wait to go back and investigate. If Becca and I were game, we could join him tomorrow as long as the weather turned.

The morning dawned bright and hot, all trace of rain clouds washed away. Summer had reached its zenith in North Carolina, weighting the air like a warm, sodden blanket. I kicked off the sheet and stretched like a cat before climbing out of bed. Padding down the hall to the kitchen, I found Mama at the stove turning bacon that hissed and popped in the iron skillet. To this day, whenever I think of my mother I picture her at that stove.

"That you, Claire?" she said without turning around.

"Mmm. Something smells good." I peeked over her shoulder at the skillet's contents. "Can I go ahead and eat?"

In reply, Mama lifted the bacon out, set it on a platter, and carried it to the table, along with a plate of scrambled eggs. "Joe Spivey was up here banging on the back door before I could get my apron tied on. Said he'd be back for you two later this morning."

"Later" turned out to be nearly lunchtime, when Joe finally materialized for the second time. "Sorry," he mumbled shyly, glancing nervously at Becca. "When you guys weren't up earlier, I went back home, and the old man put me to work." He tugged his baseball cap lower on his forehead. "You ready to go?" I reminded Becca and Joe that I still didn't know what we were going after, but my sister gave me a look that said the surprise would be worth the wait.

The backyard behind our house sloped for about 150 feet before dropping off into the woods. Oaks, maples, gum trees, poplars, sycamores, and other Southern trees formed a latticework of green overhead that blocked out the blinding sun as we walked single file down a path that zigzagged through the woods. After thirty minutes of hiking, we came to the brook.

"So where're we going?" I asked as we stepped across the log that spanned its width. Ahead, beyond the brook, the woods grew denser. I'd been in these woods many times, but we had almost reached the invisible boundary I never passed beyond. Even the trees seemed to grow taller, and the woods were darker and stiller here. Their brooding silence gave me a shiver. I knew we would soon reach the "cliff"—a sharply inclined hillside navigated by holding on to exposed roots in the red clay until you made it safely to the other side, where the ground leveled out at a higher elevation. Beyond that point, I had never ventured. But as we walked deeper into the thick foliage, Joe made it clear our destination was on the far side of the cliff. Without a word, he led us across the jutting mass of roots, Becca and I scuttling like crabs to reach the level ground that waited on the other side. We walked about a quarter mile farther, our breath noisy with exertion.

"Stop!" Joe called out, his right hand thrown up like a policeman's. "All right, let me just think for a minute."

"What is it?" Becca asked.

"I always get confused here because the trees look so much alike."

Becca frowned. "Trees? Joe, there's nothing *but* trees as far as you can see."

"I don't mean these trees, idiot. I mean *those* trees."

We looked where he pointed, first at one giant oak and then another about twenty feet up the path. Sure enough, the two trees could have been twins with their matching "horseback" limbs. "One of these days I'm gonna have to mark it," Joe muttered, more to himself than to us. After a few seconds he strode toward the farther tree and suddenly crashed into the thicket beyond.

"Wait a second, I thought you said we would stay on

the path the whole way!" I yelled. "Why are you going in there?"

"Because," Joe said, giving us a mischievous grin, "in there is where the surprise is. Come on, I've broken through the brush once or twice before, so it's not as bad as it looks."

Stepping through bright green bracken and across soggy fallen logs, we wound our way into a small clearing where an abandoned caretaker's cottage sat, tilting slightly on its earthen floor. The trees seemed to thin on the far side of the cottage, as if just beyond it the woods broke out into open land. Years later I would learn the cottage was accessible from that side of the woods by a remote county road.

Becca gave a low whistle. "How'd you ever find this place?"

"I was out scoutin' around last week and just stumbled on it." Joe's eyes scanned the scene and settled on something. "That's funny. Those weren't there last time."

We followed his line of sight to a makeshift clothesline, which sagged with the weight of two frayed towels and a bedsheet. The house was inhabited.

"You mean somebody lives here?" I hissed. "What if it's some crazy lunatic?"

Joe frowned, ignoring my whispers. "One thing's for sure—if it is a man, he sure wears funny clothes. Look." He pointed to an old-fashioned paisley dress that hung from the far end of the clothesline, half obscured by a faded green towel.

"A lady! You mean to tell me a lady lives up here? Where's her husband? Doesn't she have a family?" Becca's questions spoke for me as well.

Joe shrugged. "How would I know? I haven't exactly gone up to the door and introduced myself. But maybe that's just what I'll do. No sense snooping around this place forever without finding out who lives here."

"Are you nuts?" I grabbed his arm as he stepped forward. "We could get in trouble. Let's go home, Joe—now!"

"Not without at least one little peek. I didn't shove all the way through those woods for nothing."

Shaking his arm free, Joe edged up to the front of the cottage, crouching low as he neared two small windows that framed the door. He stretched up until he could see inside the nearest window, which was fringed by a makeshift curtain.

"There's nothing too spooky here," he mumbled against the windowpane. "Just some old—"

Becca's scream cut his words short, and I turned to stare in the direction she pointed.

Just beyond the edge of the clearing two eyes, surrounded by a tangle of graying hair, peered at us through the branches of a sycamore tree.

5

Gideon, North Carolina
June 1977

The moment our eyes registered the craggy face of the old woman she disappeared, hiding behind the tree's stout trunk.

"Hey, we already seen you!" Joe shouted. "Come on out and show your face. We ain't scared of a old lady." He took a step toward the sycamore tree in a show of bravado.

"Joe, you sure you know what you're doing?" I hissed at him, but it was too late. With a rustle of underbrush and snapping twigs, the old woman emerged from her hiding place, staring us down like the Grim Reaper. Though pulled back in a loose knot, her frizzy graying hair resembled a handful of Spanish moss thrown haphazardly over her head.

"We're sorry, ma'am, we didn't know anybody lived here," Becca blurted before I could speak. "Honest, we never meant to intrude on your property."

The old woman merely stared back at us in silence. I couldn't read the expression in her eyes, but I wasn't too eager to stick around and find out what it meant. Grabbing Becca's forearm, I started backing away from the clearing that marked the cottage's boundaries.

"We'll be on our way now. Sorry to disturb you," I said, still taking cautious backward steps with Becca in tow.

She shook her arm free of my grasp. "Hey, wait a minute, guys," Becca said, motioning me to stop. "I think we should make introductions. She's probably just as scared as we are."

My sister strode up to the old woman and extended her hand. "I'm Rebecca Ruth Trowling, and this is my sister, Claire, and our neighbor, Joe Spivey. It's awfully nice to make your acquaintance. Have you lived out here for very long?" Despite her courteous gesture, I could see Becca's legs shaking.

Joe gave me an "Is she for real?" glance, then chose that moment to say the worst possible thing he could have come up with.

"Hey, are you that witch I've heard rumors about?"

"Joe!" Becca gasped.

"Tommy Fryling bet me a week's worth of milk money that there was a real witch living in these woods, but I didn't believe him. Then he told me to prove him wrong, so that's why I came hiking out this far in the first place. Boy, he won't believe this!"

His face a picture of unabashed excitement, Joe turned

to me for support. Though I said nothing, I had heard the rumors too of a strange old woman seen around Gideon from time to time. A few local kids insinuated that she might even be distantly related to Becca and me, but when I asked Mama about it she shook her head and said that in a town this small everyone was distantly related somehow or other.

"Witch, huh?" the woman said at last. "So is that what they call me? Maybe it's just as well . . . and maybe they're right." She fixed Joe with her pale eyes, and I could practically hear his heart thumping from where I stood. I knew he'd get a lot of mileage out of this story.

"And as for you, young lady, I'm pleased to make your acquaintance too." She addressed Becca with a thin smile. "You can call me Gretchen." Her eyes took in all three of us before she started for the door of the cottage. "Come along then. I'll make a pot of tea. Don't worry, I only bite if I haven't had my breakfast."

Becca didn't hesitate at all, so Joe and I followed her to the door of the cottage—he out of curiosity, I in dread fear of leaving my baby sister alone with the old woman, polite though she seemed. The door creaked on its hinges as Gretchen pushed it open and stood back for each of us to enter. I had a fleeting thought of Hansel and Gretel trapped in the witch's oven but brushed it aside as childish nonsense.

Inside, the cottage's one room was surprisingly cozy. Several couch cushions that obviously doubled as a bed stretched along one wall, atop what looked like a homemade cotton batting mattress. A neat wooden table with two cane-back chairs stood in the center. The old woman had even placed a small clump of dogwood blossoms on the table. On the wall opposite the cushions stood an outdated cookstove, a kettle and cooking pot sitting on top.

Joe gave a low whistle, but I spoke before he could say something stupid again. "You've made it very homey in here, Mrs.—"

"Gretchen, please. Just call me Gretchen," the old woman said. "Make yourselves comfortable while I put on the tea. Go ahead, please take a seat." She gestured to the couch-bed.

Joe grabbed a chair before Becca or I could, so we settled on the cushions and tried to fill up the sudden awkward silence. Becca cleared her throat and made small talk with Gretchen, asking far too many questions in my opinion, but nobody could fault Becca for being shy once she got over her initial trepidation.

Moments later, as we sipped steaming cups of tea—witch's brew, Joe mouthed to me—I let my eyes wander to a dark corner I hadn't noticed when we first entered the cabin, a sort of nook cut into the wall that held a dressing table with a lace doily and an ornate wooden box on top. An old-fashioned black telephone sat on the table. A tarnished mirror reflected the image of the old woman, who sat across the room at the table. I started when I saw the image, unprepared for the mirror to be there. A faded sepia photograph of a young woman in a dark dress stared back from the dressing table. I turned my head away, uncomfortable in her frozen gaze.

"So just remember not to believe every rumor you hear," Gretchen was saying, her eyes pinning Joe when she said the word *rumor*.

"But how'd you come to live way out here?" Joe wanted to know. "Ain't it kinda strange for a old lady to live all alone in the woods? I mean, it might be cool if I did it, sort of like Davy Crockett, but I can't see why a lady, even if she is ol—"

He caught himself at Becca's glare.

"The answer to that question would take longer than you have time for right now, young man, so let's save it for another visit, shall we?" Gretchen rose to collect our empty cups, each a delicately patterned china. "People aren't always what they appear to be. I was young once too, you know, full of spit and vinegar like you are. But fortune had other plans for me." She gazed out the tiny window with the dishrag curtain while she spoke, and I took this as our cue to leave. Becca was fully entranced by now and bursting with more questions, I could tell. She asked Gretchen for a second cup of tea and was rewarded with another round of conversation from our elderly hostess.

After what seemed like half an hour longer, I told Becca we ought to be getting back home, and Joe sprang to his feet, obviously relieved to be going now that the adventure was past. No doubt Becca's chitchat with Gretchen bored him, and I couldn't really blame him. They had seemed to strike up a conversation meant only for two, weaving a spell of fascination around themselves while Joe and I endured the wait until we could be on our way.

Joe and I said our good-byes and pushed back through the squeaky door. Outside in the clearing, he kicked at a clod of dirt while I kept glancing back, sure Becca would follow any second. But the seconds turned into minutes, and still I could hear the murmur of their voices inside.

"What is she doing in there?" I squinted up through the trees and saw that the sun had moved farther to the west than I realized. We'd been gone a long time. "Mama'll have a fit if we're not home by suppertime."

"So will I," Joe said with a grin. He had a knack for finagling dinner at our house, then going home for a second supper. "I'm about starved as it is. That tea just made me hungrier."

At the sound of Becca's voice in the doorway I turned in time to see her slip something into her jeans pocket before holding out her hand in a polite farewell. Gretchen shook her hand and then waved to us over Becca's head. "Now that you know where I live, come back and visit sometime, children. It gets dreadful lonesome out here by myself."

"We will, ma'am," I promised as I took Becca by the hand and led her back the way we came through the thicket, but I was not sure it was a promise I would keep.

We were silent for most of the trek back through the

woods, each affected in our own way by the encounter with the old woman. I had questions I wanted to ask Becca, but not in Joe's hearing. When at last our backyard came into view through the trees up ahead, Joe cleared his throat and said he'd shove on back home—supper at our house apparently forgotten. With barely a nod, he cut off the main path down a shortcut that led to his own backyard.

Becca and I trod ahead in silence until we reached the house. After supper, we cleaned up the kitchen and headed to our room. I settled cross-legged on my twin bed, facing toward Becca's own bed with matching blue chenille bedspread, where she lay sprawled, staring up at the ceiling.

"So talk to me. What are you thinking?" I prodded. "You and that old lady really seemed to hit it off. What did she give you?"

"She has a name, Claire—it's Gretchen, remember?"

"Sor-ry," I exaggerated, taken aback by the offended tone in her voice. "I'm just curious, that's all. You two carried on like you'd known each other all your lives. I saw you put something in your pocket when you left. Did she give you something? If so, you'd better show Mama."

"Honestly, you are nosey!" Becca practically hurled the words at me. "For your information, she didn't give me anything, and, yes, we did find a lot to talk about. You and Joe acted like she was a leper, you were so eager to get out of there."

"Well, she did seem nice and all, but those witch rumors kinda give me the creeps. Be careful, that's all I'm saying."

Becca rolled her eyes at me. "Now who's being the dramatic one? Don't worry, Claire. Just imagine the stories she could tell us! Our lives are so boring sometimes, every day the same old thing. And here we stumble onto a real, live adventure with a lost heroine, for all we know."

I stared at my sister, realizing from the gleam in her eyes that she really couldn't help herself when something caught her imagination like this. It's one of the things that made me love her so much.

Becca smiled and reached for me across the chasm between our beds, but the space was too wide. "Don't worry about me, Claire. It's not like I'm going to sneak back into the woods by myself."

But, as I found out later, that was exactly what she did.

In the middle of that night, when she thought I was asleep, Becca crept out of bed and stood in the moonlight at the window. I peeked over the edge of my covers and saw her lips moving in some sort of silent prayer. She brought an object to her lips in a brief kiss, and I saw the flash of something bright. She turned then and headed for the closet, where she rustled among our Sunday dresses. I craned my neck to see where she was hiding her treasure, but the room was too dark in spite of the moonlight. An old bureau set against the back wall of the deep closet seemed like a natural hiding place, but I didn't hear any drawers opening or closing.

She slid into her bed and was soon snoring softly. Now wide awake, I made a mental note to record Becca's strange nocturnal ritual in my diary the next morning. Underscore: What secret was my sister hiding? Or was she hiding someone else's secret? Note to self: turn the closet inside out until you find the shiny thing she hid in there.

What a peculiar day it had been.

6

Gideon, North Carolina
June 2001

I stared at the crescent moon pendant in its little velvet box and heard my brother-in-law's breath close to my ear.

"What do you think? Have you seen it before? Where would Becca get such odd jewelry? I found it when I went digging through her things in search of clues. It was lying on top of a bunch of letters she kept in her drawer." Rainey sighed the long, weary sigh of someone emotionally and mentally exhausted.

"Why did she do this to me!" he said a little too loudly. A customer at the counter glanced over. Rainey turned away for a few minutes, composing himself, while I said nothing. This was certainly not the time to offer platitudes, but I was prepared to offer a plan of action once I had time to think about the next step to take. Regardless of Becca's injunction not to look for her, I knew we were both intent on doing just that. If she really didn't want to be found, why would she go to the trouble of leaving the Skizzer note here in North Carolina? She had to know it would leave a trail marker pointing to her whereabouts.

"Rainey, let me take the pendant for now. I have seen it before, but that's not important for the present. I've got some ideas about how to start searching for Becca, but I need time to rest and think it all through. Why don't we meet for breakfast tomorrow morning and start from there? First on the agenda is a visit to my aunt."
His face was still averted, but he nodded. I gathered my purse from the table and slipped out of the coffee bar before he could compose himself enough to start another round of questions.

Back at my room, I crawled into bed and played Aunt Jess's voicemail. After a curt greeting, she informed me she was looking forward to our visit tomorrow and promised to do her best to help me find Becca. She also reminded me she was holding an estate sale of sorts that weekend, unloading some of the excess furniture and "trinkets" in the townhouse. If I wanted anything in particular she would set it aside for me, or else I could sift through the pieces myself when I arrived. Despite my exhaustion, I knew I wouldn't be able to sleep yet, my mind was so awhirl. Employing a technique I often used when plotting a story, I propped up in bed and balanced a notepad on my knee, writing down words and thoughts that came to me regarding my sister's disappearance. Once I had brainstormed for a while, I would try to connect the dots and come up with a workable game plan for Rainey and me.

I started with the date Becca had disappeared, June 3, then added the other details at random:

Hair salon?

SUV gone—gas credit card trail?

Bank account

Skizzer note, NC

Secret box, NC

Radcliffe place, NC

"Terrible and wonderful"

Gold crescent moon pendant

Marriage trouble?

Affair?

33 years old

It didn't take long to run out of ideas. By now everyone was probably whispering that Becca left Rainey for a secret lover somewhere, but I just couldn't bring myself to believe it. Despite his question in the coffee bar, I knew that neither could Rainey.

"Surely I'd have some sort of gut feeling if that were the case," he had told me before I left Florida. "Wouldn't a person have some hint, some remote idea, if they were being cheated on?" He'd shaken his head slowly, his brown eyes troubled. "No. Not Becca. I'd have known, Claire. I'd have known."

His words still echoed in my ear as the room phone rang.

"Sorry to bother you again so soon, Claire, but I had a thought. This won't take a minute, I promise."

"Don't worry, Rain. I can't sleep yet anyway. What've you got?" I set the notepad on the nightstand and scooted down to rest my head against the pillow.

"Well, we got a letter from that great-aunt of yours yesterday, and it prompted me to start thinking about her just now. Are you sure she said Becca hasn't contacted her at all?"

"Right." I waited for him to go on.

"Do you trust everything the old lady says? I mean, maybe she's covering for Becca somehow."

"Not likely, but I'll certainly consider it as a starting point. Hey, I meant to ask you something too. Did Becca clean out your bank account when she left, and has she left a credit card trail in her wake? She has to be living on something."

"Not exactly cleaned out, but she definitely took a big chunk from our savings. About five thousand dollars. So far she's left no credit trail at all. She's smart, you know."

Yes, I had to give my sister that. So she was buying all her gas and food and lodging (assuming she paid for it) with cash. But even five thousand dollars wouldn't last forever.

"Before I go, Rain, tell me, did Becca mention anything out of the ordinary in the days or weeks before she disappeared?"

"Out of the ordinary?" he repeated on the other end of the line.

"I mean anything at all. Did she mention anyone or anyplace or anything she didn't normally talk about? Or maybe something happened, like a friend she hadn't heard from in years contacted her out of the blue? Or she came across an item in the news that triggered unusual conversation? I know I'm reaching here, but anything, no matter how small, will help."

"Well, let's see. She did call to tell me she was getting her hair cut on the day she disappeared, and I thought that was rather odd—not like her to do that. She also seemed to be getting lots of mail from an old college friend lately—some girlfriend who was touring the British Isles, she said. Then there's the strange pendant, of course. I don't know how long she's had it or where it came from, but when I found it in the bottom of her lingerie drawer I got the impression it was significant somehow."

Yes, the pendant. It seemed strangely significant to me too, but I wasn't prepared to go down that rabbit trail with Rainey just yet—not until I'd done some more digging on my own.

"Now that you mention it, Claire, something a bit peculiar did occur a few nights before she left," he said. I sat up in bed again, waiting for whatever he had to say.

"I remember I woke to the sound of Becca talking in

her sleep." Rainey paused as if gathering his thoughts. "She was murmuring something over and over again—some kind of flower. Tulip maybe? Or lily? When I tried to rouse her, she just rolled over and went back to sleep."

"A flower? That was all?"

"Yes. Not much help, is it?"

"I'll tuck it away in my memory for safekeeping," I assured him. "Meanwhile, we both better try to get some sleep. See you tomorrow."

Setting the phone back in its cradle, I turned out the light, slid under the covers, and gradually let sleep overtake me.

7

Gideon, North Carolina
June 2001

As Rainey and I made the short drive to Aunt Jess's townhouse late the next morning, my thoughts reeled back to my mother's family. Now there was a colorful clan—apparently as rich with secrets as they had once been with money. All I remember about my maternal grandfather are the things Mama told me about him, like the way he would stride long-legged across his vast tobacco fields in the morning, yodeling in that powerful, beautiful way he had. His voice could carry a full mile across the waving white tops of the tobacco blossoms, or so the local legends had it. Actually these don't count as real memories since Morgan Trowling blew his brains out with a shotgun years before I was born—but it's close enough to the real thing.

Steering my car toward the historic part of town—and Grandfather Trowling's only living relative—I couldn't have known the web of lies Rainey and I were about to find ourselves entangled in. Now, with the benefit of hindsight, I can look back and nod at the obvious clues. If I don't do it, who else is going to set this story down on paper and connect all the dots that led to my sister Becca's epiphany that summer? Years ago my grandfather's grisly suicide shook the town of Gideon to its core, they say. You'd think such ancient history would have no bearing on the life of two sisters decades later. But it did, in ways I never would have expected.

When I finally brought the car to a stop on the right tree-lined street, I turned to look Rainey in the eye. "Keep your hopes up, Rain. Maybe she'll know something." He gave me a halfhearted smile as he swung open the passenger door.

I pounded on the solid oak door of the townhouse until I spotted the doorbell in the center of a lion's head, its mouth gaping. From deep inside I heard the faint buzzing of the doorbell, but no footsteps. Pressing it more impatiently, this time I got results.

"Good heavens, don't you people ever stop working?" an old woman said as the door cracked open an inch or two. I tried to peek through the crack, but it was held close by a chain-lock tethered to the door frame.

"I'm not interested in whatever it is you're selling," my aunt said. She started to close the door, but I reached out and grabbed the edge before she could shut the door.

"Aunt Jess, it's me, Claire, your niece. And this is

Becca's husband, Rainey. We were coming by to talk to you about Becca . . ."

After fiddling with the chain-lock she opened the door, and I watched as recognition flitted across my aunt's face. The decades had changed her dramatically, though she still wore her hair close-cropped in a mannish style. "Ah, so it is you. Why the dickens didn't you say so from the start? Well, don't just stand there looking foolish. Come in. I asked Roberta to prepare a luncheon for us."

Rainey cleared his throat. "Excuse me, ma'am, but Claire said you might be able to help us locate Becca. She's gone . . . missing."

"Well, do you expect to accomplish this standing at my doorstep? Come on in, I'll do my best, though I don't see how I can possibly shed light on why a young woman would leave her husband," my aunt said flatly, waving us into her sitting room as she stifled a cough.

Ignoring the barb, I plunged ahead. "Aunt Jess, how are you? It's been, what, ten years since I last saw you? Are you well? That sounds like a bad cough."

"It ought to be, since I smoked for forty years. Mystery to me how I managed to quit, but I did. Once the damage is done, however, there's only so much you can do. So, about the estate sale. Anything you want me to put aside for you? You always admired the brocade princess chairs, and the cuckoo clock will fetch a bundle if no one claims it."

"You're selling the cuckoo clock? I'd love to have the clock if it's not spoken for already, but—"

"Consider it yours. Well, then, tell me what I can do for you and Rainey. Surely you're not wanting another escort to Great Britain." She chuckled at her little joke and waited for my reply.

"No, Aunt Jess." I hesitated, formulating my words. "Becca left home a week ago. Drove off in her SUV. Nobody knows where she is. Rainey and I are certain she passed through North Carolina, and we wondered if maybe she made contact with you, but from the sound of things you're as much out of the loop as we are."

Aunt Jess remained silent for a moment. "I certainly am out of the loop, as you say. Not only has Rebecca not contacted me in the past few days, she hasn't contacted me in the past few years. At least you always remember me with a Christmas card."

"Becca doesn't mean to brush you off, Aunt Jess, she's just not good about sending cards and that sort of thing." Always running to her defense, I chided myself. Would I ever stop being my sister's keeper?

Aunt Jess sipped her tea and set the cup down loudly in the saucer. "Are you sure there's nothing else you'd like me to earmark for you from the estate sale? Any of my mother's jewelry perhaps?"

"No thanks, I—"

Jewelry. The single word put an unexpected thought into my mind.

"Aunt Jess, have you ever seen a gold pendant shaped like a crescent moon, with an inset ruby for the eye?"

I saw as well as heard my aunt's slight intake of breath. She cleared her throat to cover it up, then hesitated a beat too long in her reply. "Where in the world would I have seen such a thing? Why do you ask?"

"No reason in particular. It's not important." Rainey's eyes met mine across the room.

After an hour of small talk, the occasional question about Becca thrown in for good measure, Rainey and I took our leave. I hugged Aunt Jess at the door and promised to let her know the minute we learned any news about Becca. Her shoulders felt frail and thin in my embrace, and I had a sudden flashback of the vigorous, wiry woman who'd escorted Becca and me around England all those years ago—Aunt Jess always three or four paces ahead of us in her leggy gait.

Back in the car, I decided to let Rainey drive. As he negotiated traffic I stared into space. Our silence told me we were both thinking the same thing. My aunt did indeed know about the crescent moon pendant—more than she was willing to talk about. And somehow I knew the pendant was linked to Becca's disappearance; just how, I wasn't sure yet. I reached for my notepad in the glove compartment and circled the words "gold crescent moon pendant."

8

Gideon, North Carolina
June 2001

I watched Aunt Jess's tree-lined neighborhood grow small in the car's side-view mirror, my mind a tangle of thoughts now that we were on our own again.

"You thinking the same thing I'm thinking?" Rainey said as he steered the car back toward the town center of Gideon. I glanced at him—his brow seemed to be knit in a perpetual frown these days.

"I sure am, and I intend to make good use of Aunt Jess's unintentional revelation. In fact, I've been thinking I should do a bit of research at the library. Something's been nagging at me ever since you showed me the crescent moon pendant last night. Wanna come along?"

"I've got a better idea." Rainey drove the car into a vacant parking space along Gideon's restored Main Street. "I'll drop you at the library and then head on out to the Radcliffe place—I want to see the place for myself now that we know Becca stopped there. If it was significant for her, then it's significant to me. Does that make sense?" He looked at me for validation.

"It makes all the sense in the world, Rain. While you're out there, you should poke around the old neighborhood too, see the house where we grew up." I was sure Becca had taken Rainey there at least once before.

"All right, which way to the library?" he asked, putting the car in reverse.

"Don't bother, I can walk it from here." I grabbed my purse. "How 'bout I meet you right here, in front of the Willow Tree Café, in two hours? That should give me enough time. And if you get bored with the Radcliffe house, you can always wander Main Street until I finish at the library." After giving Rainey directions to the Radcliffe house, I waved him good-bye and walked the four blocks to the county library. It was a solid-looking building of weathered gray stone, with three floors of research possibilities.

Like other small towns, Gideon had lost a generation of citizens during the '80s, when people fled to the metropolitan hot spots like Raleigh and Charlotte. During the mid-'90s, however, a national sense of nostalgia had ignited a restoration movement, and small towns across the country were revived—many times better than they were before. City dwellers jaded on the hectic pace of the rat race suddenly found these small hamlets ideal for raising families and putting down cultural roots. Gideon was no exception. The Fine Arts Center here was famous throughout the Southeast, and the town itself had earned a name for its annual autumn art festival, which attracted some of the best artists in the country.

Inside the library I asked for directions to their illustrated books on vintage jewelry. The desk assistant walked me over to a remote row of shelves that appeared to get very little traffic. She indicated the dozen or so books on jewelry and jewelry making, then selected two from that grouping that featured vintage jewelry. I saw ancient Celtic moons and goddess jewelry, but they didn't seem close enough to the pendant I had tucked inside my purse. The books being no help, I decided to try the Internet. This time the library assistant led me to the third floor, where a row of computer carrels sat waiting in a corner. Only one other person was there, so I would have relative privacy.

"The books were no help?" she queried, seeming disappointed.

"Not really . . . I mean, they helped somewhat, but I'm looking for something specific, a particular design in vintage jewelry."

She studied me for a minute, her eyes fixed on me in an odd way. "If you run into another dead end, I'd be happy to put you in touch with a local jeweler who may be able to help you. He specializes in . . . peculiar pieces."

The crescent moon pendant was peculiar, all right. I thanked her and settled into the carrel, grateful I had nearly the whole floor to myself. I typed in the keywords "crescent moon pendants," and immediately a page full of jewelry maker links filled the screen. I sifted through a dozen or so before I got to one that looked promising. The images sprang to life on the computer screen—dragons, goddesses, ancient Gothic, pagan, and Celtic symbols. On the last page of images under the "crescent moon" tab, I saw what I was looking for.

The sterling silver moon sported a sly Mona Lisa smile and a diamond-encrusted eye. Close enough. I clicked on the image to read more. Amid the price, weight, and craftsmanship details of the pendant, I almost didn't see a small link at the bottom of the page that read "history." When I clicked on the link, a pop-up window appeared, informing me about the history of the design and its ancient Celtic lineage. All good information, I thought, but not exactly helpful. The last line of text stated that the design was copied from an original that dated to the 1500s. I printed out the page and headed back to the assistant librarian's desk. She was on the phone but nodded when she saw me, understanding my need for something further from her.

"Sorry," she said, hanging up the phone and turning to face me. "My son was having a mini-crisis at home, but the fire's been put out. So, do you want directions to the jeweler I mentioned earlier?"

"You read my mind. How much do I owe you for the printout?"

She smiled. "It's on the house, but don't tell my boss I said so. Are you familiar with downtown Gideon?"

"Are you kidding? I grew up here—at least, in the old neighborhoods surrounding Gideon—but a lot has changed since then, and I almost never make it back for a visit." I watched as she sketched a rudimentary map to the jeweler's shop—a place called the Celtic Muse.

"Oh? What brings you here this time? Visiting a relative?" The assistant librarian handed me her homemade map.

"You could say that." I tucked the map into my jeans pocket and waved good-bye. "Thanks. You've been a big help."

"I hope you find what you're looking for," she called after me as I pushed through the revolving front door.

The Celtic Muse was closed—a handmade sign on the door informed patrons it would reopen at 2:00 p.m. I glanced at my watch. It was 2:15. Apparently the proprietor liked to take long lunches. The shop would have to wait, I suddenly realized, because I was supposed to meet Rainey back on Main Street at 2:30. Ever the prompt one, he was probably already there, sitting on the hood of my car, glancing at his wristwatch every few minutes.

I walked the few blocks back to the Willow Tree Café and arrived in time to see Rainey just pulling up outside. He forced a smile when he saw me. I slid into the passenger seat with relief.

"So, how'd it go?" I ventured.

"Fine. I was going to ask you the same thing." From the look on Rainey's face, he was anything but fine, but I didn't say so.

9

Gideon, North Carolina
November 1981

Loud banging at the front door jolted me out of my sleep, and instinctively I looked across at Becca's twin bed to make sure she was there beside me. The pounding came again. I grabbed my bathrobe and ambled down the hallway past the kitchen. Where was Mama? Running my hand through my hair, I opened the door to find Joe Spivey standing there with a scowl on his face.

"Do you know what time it is?" He wrinkled his nose so that the patch of freckles scrunched even closer together.

"No, but I'm sure you're about to tell me."

"Darn right I am. It's 11:15 and dress rehearsal starts in fifteen minutes. Miss Jacoby sent me over to find you two when you didn't show up for costuming and makeup. She's about fit to be tied."

A sickening wave of realization coursed through me

as I remembered the church Thanksgiving play. Today was our last rehearsal—and the two leading ladies were still in their pajamas.

"Give me ten minutes, Joe! I promise. Tell Miss Jacoby we're on our way."

I slammed the door in his face and ran back down the hallway, yelling for Becca to get up. Ten minutes later we were pumping our bikes along the mile and a half of road between our neighborhood and the little white church where we'd been baptized as babies. As we wheeled into the red clay parking lot and slung our bikes against the giant maple tree, I suddenly remembered that Mama was working the Ladies' Guild rummage sale today. No doubt there was a note reminding us of that fact in the kitchen—only we'd never made it that far.

We creaked open the door to the fellowship hall, but there was no use trying to slink in. Sharp-eyed Miss Jacoby spotted us from across the expanse of terrazzo flooring and made a beeline for us. I didn't like the grim set of her jaw.

"Claire and Rebecca Trowling, how on earth do you expect me to launch a Thanksgiving play without my two leading ladies here? I nearly had a heart attack when Joe told me you two were still in bed!"

Joe Spivey, the rat.

I started to stammer out some excuse, but Becca interjected. "Miss Jacoby, Mama was away this morning at the rummage sale, and without her there to rustle us out of bed, why, we couldn't help ourselves—especially when you've helped to make them so cozy with those comforters you made us last Christmas." She beamed her most beguiling smile on the Sunday school superintendent. Becca could melt butter with that smile.

Miss Jacoby demurred immediately. "Well, now, since you put it that way, I guess I'll have to bite my tongue. I'll reserve what I was going to say for the next crisis. Go on, now, and get in your costumes. Claire, your pilgrim costume is in the ladies' room, but Becca, you'll have to come with me. I had to take your costume home last night to wash after Mary Beth spilled Coke on it. Follow me."

The annual church Thanksgiving play was a big deal in Gideon and the high point of Miss Jacoby's year, giving her a chance to show off her artistic flair. Every year a big crowd of people squeezed into the sanctuary—quite a turnout for us, but you had to remember that in a town this size nearly everybody was related to everybody else, however distantly, and so they came to see some little second cousin or son or daughter make their dramatic debut.

That year, the Thanksgiving after our summer trip to England, I was playing a pilgrim matron while Becca played the Indian chief's wife. Every year Becca grew in her dramatic skills, which ensured that Miss Jacoby and the school drama coach always saved a lead role for her, despite her penchant for ad-libbing.

Dress rehearsal went off without a hitch, and by midafternoon we were heading home again. As we pedaled along, rubbing saddle sores into our bottoms, Becca said, "Claire, do you think anybody will mind if I . . . embellish my role tomorrow?"

I cast a sideways glance at her. "What do you mean, embellish?" The word made me nervous. What was Becca up to?

"Oh, I don't know, I just want to make the character more interesting. The wife of an Indian chieftain should have a bit more . . . pizzazz . . . don't you think?"

I groaned inwardly, hoping Becca wouldn't fly too close to the sun, like she had the year she altered her soliloquy as Lady MacBeth and completely changed the end of the play. Sometimes her dramatic flair was out of control.

"Becca, what are you planning to do? Come on, now, admit it." We put our bikes away in the toolshed and went inside to flop on the family room couch. Mama was home now, just setting two grocery sacks on the kitchen counter.

"Don't you worry about a thing, Claire. I won't change the script—I promise."

Mama poked her head around the kitchen cabinets. "What's this all about? Did the rehearsal go all right? Come on, you two—help me put away these groceries."

"Oh, Claire's just worried I'll ruin the play tomorrow." Becca shot me a wounded look and stuck out her tongue. "But I want to make an impression. Let's just say you never know when someone special might be in the audience."

Mama and I exchanged a knowing smile. So that was it. Becca was so pretty I could hardly keep up with all the Gideon boys who mooned over her month in and month out. I'd have to scan the audience tomorrow to figure out who this new crush was.

"How'd the rummage sale go?" Becca changed the subject nonchalantly. "Were there more people this time?"

"We made four hundred dollars—up from last month—but it always gets busier the closer we get to Christmas," Mama said, her tall, lanky form framed in the archway that connected the kitchen with the den. "Maybe next month you girls can come with me." As we helped put the groceries away and prepared a light supper, I couldn't stop wondering about the surprise that was in store for us all tomorrow.

Sunday morning dawned gray and overcast, not the best weather for a Thanksgiving play, but at least this year we would be inside the sanctuary. Two years earlier Miss Jacoby had overseen the construction of an outdoor stage in the church's side lawn next to the graveyard. Though the huge maple tree created a natural canopy, it proved useless when the sky blackened with rain clouds. The resulting downpour brought an abrupt end to the play, cast and crew and audience all shrieking and running for cover inside the church.

As we pedaled up to the church, I saw cars parked along the roadside a good two blocks away, and the red clay parking lot looked like a funeral for a much-loved person was going on inside. Cars were crammed in at every possible angle, some even double-parked, blocking other vehicles.

Becca and I opened the door to the fellowship hall, and pandemonium hit us full in the face. If you've ever been backstage before a big event, you know what I'm talking about. Amid shouts of "Does anybody have a safety pin?" "My costume doesn't fit!" and "Joey tore off my feathers!" I made my way to the ladies' room to get into costume. By now I was proficient at doing my own makeup and had the routine down to a science. Becca had promised to help do makeup on the younger children, so I was free to find a quiet place to go over my lines one last time.

Sneaking up the back stairs, I peeked through a hole in the wall behind the choir loft to check out the crowd. Sure enough, about five hundred people had squeezed into the small sanctuary, some standing along the back wall and others spilling into the aisles on folding chairs. My heart thumped with stage fright.

A small Indian clomped up the stairs behind me and tugged at my pilgrim apron. "Hey, lemme see."

"Shhh, Tommy, not so loud." I hoisted him up to the eyehole. "We don't want everyone finding out our hiding place." I scanned the crowd one more time, looking for a face that might belong to my sister's newest crush, but all the faces looked familiar.

Ten minutes later we were onstage, and I gestured eloquently as I intoned my lines. I stumbled over one line, and Miss Jacoby stage-whispered my cue from the wings—or, rather, the choir loft side door. We pilgrims braved our first hard winter in the New World, sowed crops in the springtime, made friends with the Indians, and then prepared the great communal feast of Thanksgiving.

As we gathered around the massive table, the Indian chief and a leading pilgrim each gave a noble speech about the bounty of the earth and God's goodness. At the close of these speeches, everyone bowed their heads in preparation for the final prayer before we partook of the bounty spread before us.

The pianist started to play the closing number when suddenly Becca sprang to her feet and stepped to the front of the stage. Looking confused, the pianist stopped playing as my sister swept her arms about dramatically and quoted lines that froze the blood in my veins.

"Out, out, brief candle! Life's but a walking shadow, a poor player that struts and frets his hour upon the stage and then is heard no more: it is a tale told by an idiot, full of sound and fury, signifying nothing . . . My only love sprang from my only hate . . . So now I bid thee Godspeed and farewell."

Horror-stricken, I realized Becca was randomly quoting lines from her favorite Shakespearean tragedies. The smile she suddenly cast in my direction said plainly, "Nobody here knows the difference anyway," and she was probably right. With a final sweep of her arms, Becca bowed low, and the crowd burst into applause and whistling. All five hundred spectators hooted and hollered their appreciation at this amazing display of dramatic ability.

Miss Jacoby gestured wildly from the wings, cuing us to line up across the front of the stage to take our bows. We stumbled into position, still confused by Becca's unsettling turn of the script, but by all accounts the play was a huge success.

As the cheering rang in my ears, I glanced over in time to see my sister slip a pendant necklace from beneath her Indian costume. She kissed the pendant, nodded, and smiled at someone in the back of the sanctuary. I followed her gaze, expecting to see a lovesick adolescent boy with misty eyes. Instead, I saw an old woman, her face partially obscured by a hat veil. Something about the old woman looked vaguely familiar and at the same time out of place, dressed as she was in peculiar, old-fashioned clothes.

She moved her head slightly, giving me a better view of her face, and in that instant I recognized the old woman from the cottage in the woods. With one timid, gloved hand held up in a wave good-bye, she turned and slipped out the back door.

10

Gideon, North Carolina
June 2001

Rainey and I parted company at the hotel elevator, and I crashed on my hotel bed for the next two hours. Around dusk, I decided to drive out to the old Radcliffe place alone, wanting to see it again for some inexplicable reason—perhaps because the site of the sister secret box was my last tangible connection to Becca in this unlikely turn of events. Twilight had settled over the landscape when I pulled my car next to the curb in front of the old house, its twin gables casting shadows over the facade. Just beyond, a low stone wall marked the entrance to our old neighborhood, a tribute to its name, Stonewall Acres, I had always assumed. Not until I was a grown woman did I realize the neighborhood was actually named after Confederate General Stonewall Jackson. This was the South, after all.

The wind picked up as I approached the house, and a

row of blackbirds along the rooftop stared down at me with their beady eyes. I scanned the grounds, returning to the place where I'd found the pink tin box, and then moved to the edge of the woods that bordered the property. I looked up into the darkening sky and saw the moon, already a brilliant white against the indigo expanse. It occurred to me that this was a perfect time for prayer—for Becca, for Rainey, for myself—but it had been a long time since I'd prayed. The words Colin had spoken in the bell tower of the stone church floated back to me: "The right melody is like a prayer, don't you think?" But I had no melody—couldn't even remember some scrap of a hymn at the moment.

The sky was completely black by now. I breathed in the stillness that surrounded me. "If you're out there, please keep Becca safe, wherever she is. Help us to find her, God. Help us all to find our way again."

A bell tinkled when I opened the door to the Celtic Muse the next day. Aromatic smoke from burning incense created a soft gray haze in the shop, and I saw books, jewelry, pottery, and a host of other Celtic paraphernalia. From somewhere a sound system played moody Celtic music.

At the sound of the bell, a man with a long gray ponytail and bushy beard emerged from behind a curtained doorway beyond the counter.

"Welcome. I always say anyone who finds the Celtic Muse was destined to be here. Are you looking for anything special? Our pottery is half price from now till Christmas."

"No, I, well, actually I was hoping you could give me your expert opinion on something," I said, somewhat apologetically when I saw momentary disappointment in the shopkeeper's eyes at the loss of a sale. Perhaps I would buy some trinket before I left.

"That depends on what you have to show me." He settled heavily on a stool behind the counter and waited while I fished the small black velvet box out of my purse. When I opened it and he saw the gold crescent moon pendant, he gave a low whistle.

"Where'd you get this?" He reached out to hold the pendant for a closer look.

"My sister acquired it somehow, and I need to find out if it's significant in any way."

"You can say that again," the shopkeeper muttered as he set a jeweler's loupe in his eye and examined the pendant through the magnifying lens. "Did she buy this from a collector?"

"No, I believe it was a gift to her from an old woman. Why, is it valuable?"

"You can say that again," the shopkeeper repeated. "Or at least that's my first impression. Bears checking out. What exactly are you hoping to learn about this piece?"

"I'm not really sure. When it was made, where it was made, who made it—whatever you can tell me." How could I tell him I was merely following a hunch that might somehow help me find my sister? Instead I said, "How long would that kind of research take?"

But instead of answering, the shopkeeper disappeared back through the curtained doorway for several long minutes and then reemerged with a Polaroid camera. "Next best thing to examining the actual artifact," he said. "I don't suppose you'd be willing to leave the pendant in my possession for a few days? It'll take that long to research it." He looked at me, his bushy gray eyebrows raised in question.

"I could leave it with you for just a day or two, Mr.—"

"Bob, just call me Bob." He settled his bulk back onto the stool and positioned the pendant for several close-up looks with his loupe.

"Now that's interesting," I heard him say as I selected a small vase to purchase. His head was bent low over the pendant, a small penlight trained on the back of it. "Haven't seen one of these in more than a decade, but we wanna make sure it's the real thing before we start jumping to conclusions."

I returned to the counter. "Were you talking to me?"

Bob stroked his beard and grinned. "My own little vice—the wife says it's the first sign of going crazy, but I always remind her I'm way past that point." He laughed at his joke and returned his attention to the crescent moon, suddenly sober.

"Give me a couple days. That should be enough time for me to research the pendant and have an answer for you. I have some books I want to dig through, plus a colleague in the business who may prove helpful."

He leveled a steady gaze at me. "Of course, you're prepared to pay a research fee, aren't you? My time is money, as they say."

"Of course. Here's my number at the hotel."

For the next two days I got reacquainted with Gideon, strolling the downtown streets and exploring new shops that had sprouted during the past half decade of regeneration. Aunt Jess phoned once, and we chatted for a few minutes; she'd hired a boy to haul the cuckoo clock down from the attic, and it was now ready for retrieval she said, but I had resolved not to return to her house until I heard back from Bob at the Celtic Muse. As I walked Main Street I had to resist the impulse to turn down the side street that led to the hazy little shop—better to let Bob have the full weight of time and resources before delivering the verdict about the antique pendant.

While I wandered Gideon, Rainey holed up inside his hotel room, working from his laptop in between frequent calls to his office back home. On the third day the hotel phone beside my bed jangled noisily as I was heading out for another day of aimless wandering. I snatched it up.

"Hello?"

"Yeah, this is Bob over at the Celtic Muse—"

"Do you have something for me?"

"You can say that again. That pendant of yours is quite a find. How soon can you be here?"

"Ten minutes," I blurted. "But can't you tell me anything over the phone?"

"Better if you wait and see what my colleague found in a rare book—this kind of thing is best in person."

"I'm on my way." I slammed the phone down and then picked it back up to dial Rainey's room. He answered on the second ring.

"Hey, I just heard back from the guy at the Celtic shop."

"And . . . ?"

"Sounds like he's got something to tell us about the moon pendant. I think you should come with me."

"Ho, there!" a booming voice called out from the doorway of the Celtic Muse as we approached the shop. Bob swung the glass door wide to let us enter. "Come in, come in. There's someone I want you to meet."

"And there's someone I want you to meet too," I said, gesturing to Rainey. "Bob, this is my brother-in-law, Rainald Garrett." The two men shook hands, and then Bob led us behind the counter and through the curtain to a back room. I felt like Dorothy, ushered behind the veil to the Wizard's control room. Bob pulled up the ubiquitous stool before delving into whatever he had to tell us. I sneaked a glance at Rainey to catch his impression of the hazy shop. His bright blue eyes took in the madcap disarray of the Celtic Muse back office, but he remained silent.

For the first time I noticed a small man with enormous, staring eyes sitting quietly in the corner of the room.

His hands were folded in his lap, and he looked on in silence, as if awaiting his cue.

Seeing my glance, Bob gestured to the small man in the corner and made introductions. "Ah, yes, this is the colleague I was telling you about—Phineas Culver. He's a rare and antique jewelry dealer and just about the finest researcher in the business. Phineas, this is the lady I was telling you about, Ms. Trowling, and, um—"

"Rainey," my brother-in-law supplied, somewhat stiffly.

"Yes, Mr. Rainey. Well, are you two ready for a treat?" As he said these words Phineas Culver slid out of his chair and produced a large book of faded, cracked red leather. He settled it on a long table, and Rainey and I stepped closer to get a good look.

Bob let Mr. Culver lead the presentation, standing quietly behind us and breathing noisily.

Phineas Culver affixed wire reading glasses to his nose and looked over them at me. "You'll be curious to know you are only the third person I've encountered in my career as an antique jewelry dealer who possessed authentic Pritchard-Thornsby artifacts."

I must have given him a puzzled look, because he went on, seeing I was more confused than impressed. "Don't worry—the others didn't know what they had either, but believe me when I tell you the pendant is quite valuable indeed."

As his words sank in, I turned to look at Rainey beside me. His eyes barely flickered, and I knew what he was thinking: *I don't care about the cash value of the blasted pendant—just tell me how it points the way to Becca.*

Mr. Culver opened the large book gingerly and turned to a bookmarked section near the back. He smoothed his hand across the yellowed pages to flatten them better and pointed to a subheading that read "The North-Country Masters." Beside it was a woodcut image of a crescent moon pendant, a long chain looped from the top and curling back around the moon's lower curve. I recognized Becca's mysterious jewelry at once.

"That's it," I said. "Becca's crescent moon. How old is this book?"

Mr. Culver said nothing. Instead, he pulled a magnifying glass from a silk pouch hidden in his breast pocket and held it over the image on the yellowed page.

"Ah, but don't miss the most important aspect of what I'm showing you," he said in his crisp English accent, ignoring my question. "Look there, in the bottom right-hand corner of the woodcut."

As he held the magnifying glass in place, I bent low over the musty-smelling book and gazed at a peculiar insignia—what looked like an ornate rendering of the letters P and T entwined. The script trailed off in a loop that mirrored the placement of the pendant chain beneath the crescent moon.

I could hear Rainey breathing close to my ear. A clock ticked somewhere in the cluttered room, and instinctively I glanced up at Bob. His eyes shone, and he nodded wordlessly.

Mr. Culver gestured to the insignia and cleared his throat. "Samuel Pritchard and Alister Thornsby are considered by most serious antiquities dealers to be among the greatest Celtic craftsmen of the Renaissance but largely forgotten by the mainstream junk dealers who pass for professionals in today's rare jewelry market. When Robert first told me about the pendant you possess, I doubted it was the genuine artifact, but he insisted he had inspected it, and knowing him to be an astute Celtic historian as well as a sharp-eyed jeweler, I decided to give him the benefit of the doubt. So much so that I flew here last night to see the pendant for myself."

Mr. Culver gazed at the pendant in its black velvet box for a moment before lifting it out. He turned the gold pendant over and ran his index finger along the bottom edge of the crescent moon.

"You see, there it is," he said, more to himself than to anyone else in the room. Rainey and I exchanged a perplexed glance as the English jeweler put a loupe to his eye and examined the pendant under a light.

"Robert, I daresay you won't see another one of these in the next twenty years, especially in this outback you call a town."

The jewelers seemed to forget about us as they gazed at the pendant, muttering jeweler talk between themselves.

Rainey cleared his throat. "Other than their rarity, can you provide us any information about the pendant?

Trust me when I say an awful lot might hinge on what you tell us."

The two jewelers looked up from the table as if surprised we were still there. Culver motioned us over to the book.

"It's all right there, anything you might want to know about Pritchard and Thornsby and their signature design. But, to spare you a long read, I can tell you that these two master craftsmen created only a few dozen pieces of jewelry before their untimely deaths. They're called the North-Country Masters because they lived in a small Yorkshire town in the north of England—a place called Kellerby."

I looked up at Culver, startled to hear the name of the town Becca and I had visited as girls with Aunt Jess. "Did you say Kellerby?"

Phineas Culver took off his reading glasses and tucked them away before answering. "That's right. The town has a long history of Celtic and Druidic influences. Do you know it?"

All three men turned to stare at me while I found my tongue. "Know it—my goodness, this is uncanny. I visited England when I was fourteen, and to this day Kellerby stands out as the most vivid of my memories from the UK."

I slowly became aware that Rainey was staring at me hard, and I turned to meet his gaze. His dark curly hair looked ruffled in the half light of the back room, but it was the look in his eyes that brought me up short.

Phineas Culver snapped open a briefcase and drew out a checkbook. "I'm prepared to make you a handsome offer on the pendant, Ms. Trowling. You are the owner of it, I presume."

"No, she's not." Rainey stared at the little man. "It belongs to my wife, and it's not for sale." He held out his hand so that Culver was obliged to return the gold pendant.

"But you haven't heard my offer yet, Mr.—"

"I'm not interested in your offer. The pendant is not for sale," Rainey repeated. "It has sentimental value, and at the present even more than that."

Rainey tucked the black velvet box in his pocket. As he muttered another "excuse me" and headed back through the curtain, I turned to Bob and asked him how much I owed him for his research. He and Culver both looked annoyed at having lost the opportunity to purchase the jewelry, but Bob recovered himself enough to name a fee. I wrote him a check, and he produced a sheaf of papers about Pritchard and Thornsby. Glancing at them, I guessed that most were photocopies from Culver's red leather book, but I saw a handful of other pages included in the stack.

Culver had fixed his large eyes on me, and I shifted uncomfortably while I said polite good-byes and thanked both men for taking the trouble to research the pendant.

"By all means, I hope you can prevail upon your brother-in-law to reconsider," Phineas Culver said as he shook my hand rather stiffly. "Artifacts like these shouldn't remain hidden away. If he needs prompting, tell him I'm prepared to offer a figure in the six-digit range."

I looked at the slight man before me and shook my head. "I'm afraid no amount of money is enough to persuade Rainey at the present, Mr. Culver, but I will take your card. A little time may change things."

The corner of his mouth twitched in a half smile, and he gave a curt nod. "Well, then, I guess our business is concluded for the present."

I tucked the sheaf of papers under my arm, gathered up my purse, and ducked through the curtain back into the main shop area, then out the front door.

11

Gideon, North Carolina
June 2001

I caught up with Rainey half a block up the street, pacing in front of a bookstore's long display window. Hailing him like a cab, I linked my arm through his and steered us down to the corner and then right onto Main Street. The Willow Tree Café had an outdoor gazebo with a smattering of tables, and I knew just the one I wanted right now.

"Good, it's empty," I said, thinking out loud as I spied the last table in the back. A wrought-iron railing smothered in jasmine ran along the side of the gazebo, separating it from a fragrant alley the local merchants had turned into a secret garden. Settling into my chair, I placed the sheaf of papers on the table and looked at Rainey.

His glance took in the papers and then me. "Helpful, I hope. That creepy little Brit was starting to get on my nerves."

I ignored his remark. "There's a mound of information here about the crescent moon jewelry. We might uncover something important—"

"Claire, that English town he mentioned . . ."

"Kellerby?"

"Yeah, that's the one. Those letters I told you about that Becca's been getting lately from some friend in England? Well, they're all postmarked from Kellerby."

Now it was my turn to stare in silence. I'd momentarily forgotten about the letters Rainey said Becca had been receiving from a "friend" in England over the past several months. Just then the waitress came and took our order. Several minutes passed before we could pick up the trail of our conversation again. I reached across the table and grabbed Rainey's wrist for emphasis.

"No wonder your eyes turned as big as saucers when Culver said the word Kellerby!"

"Exactly." Rainey wiped his mouth with a napkin and leaned forward, his forearms leaning on the table. "The return address is always the same."

"Rainey, do you know how many letters Becca received from England?"

He shook his head. "Maybe five or six."

I stirred my iced tea and thought for a minute. Earlier Rainey had told me he found the letters in the same lingerie drawer as the crescent moon pendant. "Why don't you ask Millie to overnight them to you?" Millie was a retired schoolteacher who lived next door to Becca and Rainey, entrusted with a spare key to their house. "Those letters might tell us what we need to know right now. We can apologize for snooping later."

Rainey nodded as he took a spoonful of his minestrone soup. "That's not a bad idea." He flipped open his cell phone to dial his neighbor.

We ate in silence for the next several minutes, and once the dishes were cleared away I placed the sheaf of papers on the table. Separating out the ones that looked extraneous to those photocopied from the leather book, I handed them to Rainey. Aside from an occasional horn honking and the trickle of water from a fountain in the alley courtyard, the gazebo was quiet. Only one other couple sat outside, and their table was several feet away, close to the Main Street sidewalk. They murmured soft words to each other and seemed oblivious to anything around them. Good. I shifted in my chair to find a more comfortable position and started reading.

"The North-Country Masters, Samuel Pritchard and Alister Thornsby, earned that title over the comparably short period of years in which they crafted jewelry from their goldsmith shop in Kellerby, Yorkshire. From 1550 to 1563 the artisans created the signature design of their goldsmithy, the Celtic Crescent Moon, known for its distinct facial features and delicate rendering. During the thirteen years of its existence, the smithy produced numerous pieces of jewelry, including a dozen rare artifacts commissioned by a royal containing jewels from the monarch's private vault. All but three of the ruby Crown crescents were lost to antiquity."

I paused and looked up at Rainey. "Get this. Pritchard and Thornsby were crafting jewelry while Queen Elizabeth was on the throne."

"Good stuff," Rainey answered with a slight smile. I could tell he was trying to humor me, so I answered his smile with one of my own and continued reading.

Several paragraphs of tedious detail about the goldsmithy followed, including an extract about the making of gold jewelry in the sixteenth century. I started skimming. Seven paragraphs down, a name caught my eye.

"The nature of Samuel Pritchard's death is the subject of vigorous dispute. . . . Following Pritchard's death, Thornsby carried on the business with the help of an apprentice, one Chastain Lockwood, said to be the illegitimate son of Pritchard's mistress . . ."

I looked up. "Well, did you catch it?"

Rainey blinked and waited for me to elaborate.

"Lockwood. Didn't Becca ever tell you about that trip we took to England when we were girls?"

I didn't wait for his answer but plowed on. "We stayed at this old gothic Rectory bed and breakfast in Kellerby, and the surname of the proprietor was Lockwood—Eugenia Lockwood."

We sat quietly again for a few minutes until I broke the silence. "Another link to Kellerby. How long ago did you say Becca started receiving those letters?"

"Four or five months. Yes, that sounds about right because it was just after New Year's Eve. I remember because some kids did a drive-by mailbox bashing and the mailman had to hand deliver our mail for a couple of days before I put a new box up. Becca usually picked up the mail, but I happened to be home that day and saw the letter but didn't think anything of it."

"Are you sure it was the first one? When were the others postmarked, the ones you found in her lingerie drawer?"

The waitress brought our bill, and Rainey gave her his credit card. "The night Becca left, I went crazy searching the house for a reason why, and I saw the bundle of letters but honestly didn't pay any attention to them. She had already told me an old friend from school was writing her. I'm pretty sure the one that arrived the day after New Year's was the first one."

I soaked in his words while my mind played back over the conversation with Aunt Jess a few days ago. Her eyes had dilated when I mentioned the crescent moon pendant, and it was obvious she knew more than she wanted to tell—at least up to that point.

I grabbed my purse and stood up. "It's time to pay Aunt Jess that second visit I've been waiting for. Now I think we're armed with enough information to prod her a bit more."

Back on the street we turned west into the afternoon sun, our steps quicker now that we had a sense of where to look next. As we approached the intersection that led to our hotel, Rainey hooked right a few paces before he realized I wasn't following him.

"Aren't you coming back to the hotel?" He ran his

hand through his shaggy dark hair. "You need the car if you're going to visit your aunt again."

"I will, but first I want to do a bit more digging at the library. This time in the genealogy section." I winked at Rainey. "If there are skeletons in the family closet, I want to know about them before I tackle Aunt Jess again."

12

Gideon, North Carolina
June 2001

The truth was, I wanted to be alone right then to think—and to go over the Pritchard and Thornsby papers some more—before I went back to the library. It was one of those rare summer days with a sky blindingly blue. Young mothers pushing strollers with toddlers in tow ambled along the sidewalks, window shopping and eating ice cream cones from Lita's Divine Creamery at the intersection of Broadman and Lexington. In its restoration campaign the city council had turned the entire next two blocks, between Lexington and Pickering, into a town park bordered by bushy oak trees. A children's playground sat at one end of the park, and winding paths twined among stout azalea bushes just starting to bloom throughout the rest of the grounds.

I'd noticed the park on my first trip to the library. It looked like a good place to think and get lost in for a while. When I'd grown tired of reading, I would walk the three blocks to Webster, where the library was located midway down to the right.

A mother pushing two young children on a swing looked up as I walked by, the white pebbles of the park path crunching noisily under my feet. I nodded hello and headed for a vacant bench near the shady side of the park. I decided on a bench nestled in a grove beside the park fountain. Plopping the sheaf of papers on the bench beside me, I leaned back and closed my eyes. A swarm of random thoughts and images flitted through my mind—a young Becca holding up the sister secret box for me to see; Colin Lockwood squinting up at me as he planted flowers in the ground; a pint-sized Aunt Jess waving Becca and me back to the inn from her distance up the dirt road; the unsettling face of a devil leering out from the crumbling stone wall of a church; a crescent moon pendant lying on a bed of cotton in a black velvet box.

I picked up the sheaf of papers, rereading more thoroughly what I'd perused at the café with Rainey. Absorbed in my reading, I didn't notice the sun's steady glide toward the western horizon until a glance at my watch informed me I'd better get to the library soon. Gathering my things, I hurried to the library and scanned my temporary card at the counter. The assistant librarian looked up from her computer screen and smiled a greeting. "Oh, it's you again."

"How late are you open tonight?"

"You have about two hours, but if you plan to do any serious digging I'd get started right away. Need any help, you know where to find me."

I smiled my appreciation and headed for the genealogical room on the second floor. I drew out a notepad and made a list of the names—both person and place names—I wanted to research. After much digging I traced the first Lockwood from Kellerby, England, to settle in America—one Charles Lockwood who took his new bride to Edenton, North Carolina, following the cholera epidemic of 1849.

Right state, I thought, and kept reading.

Charles's sister Mariah followed him a year later and took a husband from a prominent North Carolina tobacco family, a young man barely twenty—Thomas Davenport Trowling. I nearly lurched in my seat. Scanning through the generations, I soon discovered that Thomas and Mariah's descendants a hundred years later included a Morgan Meriwether Trowling—my grandfather and Aunt Jess's brother. His wife, Dorothea Trowling, nee Sanderson, was the grandmother I had never met and knew very little about. My mother told me she died of some vague illness, but one time when I mentioned this to Aunt Jess she snorted and muttered something about veiling the truth from children.

Left motherless as a toddler, Mama was raised largely by her nursemaid and Aunt Jess, who was already considered a spinster by the time her sister-in-law Dorothea died in 1952.

Struck with a sudden thought, I decided to look up copies of the *Gideon Post-Dispatch* in the microfiche department. Placing the film under the microfiche lens, I started sifting through the weeks and months of the newspaper's editions. The Trowling family had been prominent in its heyday, before my grandfather's suicide in 1953, but even in the years following his death their holdings remained considerable. Most people credited Aunt Jess's shrewd business head. She ran the tobacco business as well as managed Grandfather's various real estate investments. I expected to run into lots of stories about the Trowlings, and I did. An index search produced more than five hundred entries—stories about Gideon city council meetings, business transactions, speeches given, debutante balls, tobacco harvesting accidents, births and deaths . . .

Births and deaths—that might be a good thing to check out. Aside from the obvious front-page news story about Morgan Trowling's horrific suicide, I scanned birth and death announcements until my eyes fell on something that warranted my special attention. It was an obituary on Dorothea Trowling, my grandmother. The obituary said she "died of exposure." But that wasn't what made my breath catch in my throat; the final sentence of the obituary gave her full name: Dorothea Gretchen Trowling. My grandmother's middle name was a name I could never forget, etched as it was on my memory from the summer of the sister secret box and the old woman in the woods. Seeing her name on the printed page all but confirmed a hunch I'd harbored for more than twenty years—that the old woman named Gretchen had indeed gifted my sister with the crescent moon pendant, a pendant that had likely found its way into the Lockwood family from England. It also nearly confirmed something else—that Gretchen was my grandmother, and Becca's too. I knew just the person who could provide me with answers. Reaching in my handbag, I pulled out my cell to call Aunt Jess.

13

Gideon, North Carolina
November 1981

I pedaled hard to catch up with Becca, already a block ahead and careening around a corner. She kicked her legs out playfully, letting the bicycle coast along as she threw a loud giggle over her shoulder at me. Her eyes were shining; that much I could see even from this distance. No doubt she was proud of that showstopper of a stage finish she'd delivered at the Thanksgiving play. Afterward, all five hundred of us ate dinner on the grounds until our seams were ready to burst, and I kept my eye on Becca, sure she would make her way to the old woman I'd seen at the back of the sanctuary. But the woman was gone.

Mama drove by at a crawl, honking and waving, the Fairlane's front seat stuffed with our costumes and grocery sacks full of Corningware crusted with leftovers. "Last one home's a rotten egg," she called out, then accelerated to give me a good race. I was red-faced and panting by the time I slung my bicycle in the toolshed and went inside to find Becca. Mama was putting the dirty dishes in the sink to soak. She looked up at me and smiled as I came in.

"You, young lady, delivered a stunning performance. I'm so proud of you, Claire." She dried her hands on a dishrag and kissed me on the cheek. "Why don't you and your sister have a nap now. It's been a long day for you—up since dawn and your nerves probably shot to pieces from stage jitters."

"Where is Becca anyway—already flopped in bed?"

Mama smoothed the hair back from her brow and turned to find another chore. "I'm not sure, sweetie. She breezed in here right behind me, said a curt hello, and then headed down the hall. She's at that age, you know."

But Becca was not in our bedroom, nor holed up in the bathroom soaking in one of her hour-long beauty baths. I was about to check the basement when something made me stop. The window on Becca's side of the room was cracked open, the white chiffon Priscilla curtains billowing in a lively dance. It was too chilly out for open windows this time of year. Edging closer, I saw that Becca had placed a small black velvet box on the windowsill. Inside the hinged box the crescent moon pendant grinned up at me. I had not seen the odd jewelry since she first showed it to me at the old Radcliffe place four years ago.

As I lifted the pendant out a small piece of paper

fluttered to the floor. Becca had folded it into a tiny square. Inside the note said, "Follow the man in the moon to the Radcliffe house. I'll be waiting," signed with her signature smiley face.

Changing into blue jeans and a cable-knit sweater, I tucked the black velvet box under Becca's pillow, mumbled some excuse to Mama, and headed out on foot to the abandoned house at the front of our neighborhood. The old house with its shuttered facade always filled me with a creepy vibe I both loved and dreaded. The neighborhood boys had broken out two upstairs windows, giving the black holes the appearance of wide, staring eyes.

I called her name and waited. No response came, so I called again and circled to the back of the property, the plot feeling oddly empty with the blackbirds all gone south for the approaching winter. Scanning the backyard, I saw the outhouse with its crazy tilt and nearly let my eyes pass it by. The door of the outhouse featured a crescent-moon cutout, the old symbol denoting "boys only" that I'd seen a thousand times before but now looked at with sudden recognition. Becca's man in the moon.

Creaking open the door, I was thankful long decades of abandonment had dissipated any odor from the outhouse. On the inside of the door my sister had thumbtacked a piece of notebook paper with a large arrow pointing back toward the house. As I ripped the paper off I heard a stifled laugh from inside the house. Glancing up

I saw her pale face at the broad bay window of the dining room. She gestured for me to come inside and then pulled back out of sight, into the house's dark interior.

"Becca, enough of your games. What d'you want?" I crumpled the notebook paper inside my fist and strode toward the back door. It wasn't often we ventured inside the house, haunted as it was claimed to be, but we were older now and beyond such childhood fantasies. I pushed the door open and stepped through the dilapidated kitchen to the dining room. The crystal chandelier sat in a heap of dust and cobwebs on the floor, having long ago dropped from its lofty height. Faded wallpaper still clung to the water-stained walls in strips. Ornate furniture, broken up over time to fuel the braver neighborhood kids' fires, hinted at the room's long-ago elegance.

"Becca?" I stepped past the clutter through the archway that led to the drawing room and finally found her across the foyer in a small room that probably served as a ladies' parlor a century ago. I stopped short when I saw the guest sitting sedately beside her at a small table Becca had covered with Mama's best lace tablecloth. It was the old woman from the woods.

"Oh, you're not alone." The words came out too abrupt sounding, so I smiled to cover my rudeness.

Becca jumped in. "Claire, do you remember Gretchen from our visit to the woods four years ago? She came to see my performance in the play today. Actually, she's been giving me drama tips for some time now." Becca tossed a shy smile at her companion. "I wanted you two to get reacquainted before she has to go back home. Jeb, the clerk from Binder's Grocery, will come to fetch her before sundown. He gives her rides into town and back whenever she needs to come here."

I gave Becca a meaningful look. So she had visited the cottage in the woods again, many times by the sound of it. And despite her promise otherwise. I wondered how she had managed to fool me for so long.

"Yes, come join us for a belated tea, Claire." Gretchen patted the overturned crate next to her at the table, a single votive candle burning at its center. "It's not often I get to visit with two such delightful guests. You were wonderful in the play too, my dear."

"Yes, but I was magnificent," Becca trilled as she leaped up and pirouetted around the room, posturing and posing and sweeping her arms out in grand gestures. Gretchen laughed and clapped her hands, calling out "Brava! Brava!" which only spurred Becca on.

"All right now, enough of that," Gretchen said as Becca collapsed breathless in her chair again, tossing a triumphant smile at me.

"Isn't she fabulous, Claire? Gretchen coached me in my stage movements."

I took the small paper cup filled with Kool-Aid that Gretchen proffered and turned to Becca. "When did you find time for all these practices? You must have paid a visit to Gretchen at least a dozen times." I felt oddly betrayed somehow, as though her sneaky trips into the woods had broken some trust-bond between us as sisters.

Becca looked wounded and about to retort something, but Gretchen interjected, "Not quite that many, but perhaps half as much. I wish you could have come too, Claire. But, please, let's talk of other things. My time is limited, as Rebecca said, and you two are going away soon. I don't know when I might see you again."

"I told her about Mama's new job in Florida," Becca filled me in. "Thought it would be a good idea to get us all together for this farewell tea."

So that's what this was. Our mother had accepted a good-paying job in central Florida, it was true, and we had six weeks to pack up the house and move all our treasures—all our lives—to a distant place I could never think about without envisioning palm trees and pink flamingos on postcards. Looking back and forth between Becca's still-flushed face and Gretchen's inscrutable one, I realized they were waiting for a response from me. I felt like the odd one out in this strange little gathering, the backdrop of ruins all around us. And yet for all its strangeness it felt important somehow—the kind of moment that crystallizes in time and stays with you long afterward.

I sipped the bright red Kool-Aid and set my paper cup back on the table, not knowing what else to say about the matter. "So what did you two want to talk about? Shouldn't we take you back to the house and let you meet our mother?"

"No, no, I'm afraid there's no need for that." Gretchen reached inside a clutch purse on her lap. "I have something I want to give each of you—to help you remember me by." She handed me an old-fashioned drawer sachet with tiny flowers embroidered on it. Becca's gift was a miniature picture frame containing a black-and-white photo of Gretchen as a young woman. In the picture she stood against the trunk of a massive tree with a tire swing, her calf-length skirts exposing clunky-heeled shoes.

Sitting on our makeshift chairs, we told her what was going on in our young lives and listened as she reminisced about her own childhood in western North Carolina, where she grew up on a farm with free run of the surrounding hills. She told us of her love affair with the stage—her introduction to drama through a school play—but cut the story short when she reached her young adult years and started acting professionally.

Time passed quickly, and as the afternoon light started to fade we heard a car idling at the curb. Gretchen stood to her feet. "I think my ride is here, ladies. Thank you for this farewell tea, my dears. Promise me you'll write."

Gretchen picked her way through the rubble to the back door, the only entrance still passable. We followed her to the curb, then stood quietly as the Binder's Grocery clerk helped her into the car. Before they drove away she looked at us, her eyes filled with sadness.

"Once you find out who you are, don't ever let it go. Promise me that. You don't want to live someone else's idea of what your life was meant to be." She blew us a kiss, and I let her words sink in as we watched the car move down the road and out of sight.

14

Gideon, North Carolina
December 1981

One night the wind came up through the hollow beside our house, rattling windowpanes and throwing tree branches into a delirium. In that blinking half-witted state between sleep and wakefulness I knew winter had come. Minutes, or perhaps hours, passed and I floated along in a dreamscape with the howling wind for a score. But somewhere toward morning my mind registered quiet—a silence so deep it blankets everything in its path. Before I crept to the window I knew what I would find: snow.

Becca snored softly in her bed, a breathy rhythmic sound so familiar it had become a permanent backdrop to my nocturnal childhood. I crept to her bedside and nudged her shoulder until she rolled over and demanded to know what I wanted. "Becca, it's snowing outside."

Without a word she clutched her comforter around her, the long end dragging the floor like a cape, and rushed to the window beside me. We pressed our noses against the freezing glass the way we had done when we were little and laughed then shushed one another so as not to spoil the ambience.

The Thanksgiving play was two weeks behind us—Christmas approaching fast—and winter proper should have been another month away. But a winter that steals in during the dead of night trailing snow in its wake is always magical, and most welcome to the young. As I recall it now, that was the last Christmas Becca and I were capable of being enchanted in a childlike sense of the word. Too old to be kids yet too young to be women. I remember that Christmas for another reason too.

School closed early for the holidays, the roads nearly impassable as the silent snow continued to fall. Huge windswept drifts collected against houses and tree trunks and trash cans—almost anything perpendicular to the ground. Joe Spivey pounded on our front door and lodged a snowball in my face the moment I opened it. His action demanded a rematch, and so Becca and I spilled out of the house flailing arms and hurling snowballs amid shouts and bursts of laughter. We fell on the ground like toddlers and made snow angels, intoxicated with the magic of our snowbound landscape. Twilight comes early on snowy days. Pushed inside by the fading light, Becca and I went our separate ways—me to my twin bed to read, she to Mama's room to talk to a boy on the phone.

The days leading up to Christmas that year passed in a slow, whitewashed haze, and we quickly grew bored with our no-school routine. It didn't take long to run out of card games or snowball fights or reruns of our favorite TV shows or even books. As the snow piled up around our redbrick house, closing us in with an eerie quiet, I glanced at the calendar and begged for Christmas to come early. Mama put us to work baking pies and cookies shaped like stars and candy canes, sprinkled with a generous portion of green and red sugar crystals.

We drove to Grauman's Christmas Tree Lot just outside downtown Gideon and selected a balsam fir for the living room. The trunk was slightly bent, but you could disguise the imperfection by tilting the tree at a particular angle—and the crooked trunk knocked a few dollars off the price, something Mama was always looking to do. Since we had no man in the household, Mr. Grauman was kind enough to haul the tree to our Fairlane and bind it to the roof with twine. We honked as we pulled out of the tree lot, snowflakes creating a surreal effect on the windshield and the slap-slap of the wipers so loud we had to talk above them. Sitting in the front seat beside Mama, I was nearly mesmerized by the white fairy world outside our car windows.

"Do you ever remember a winter like this?" I glanced over. Mama was hunched forward in the driver's seat to get a better view of the road. She seemed not to hear me. I tried again. "I mean, this snow is incredible—ridiculous almost. Did it ever snow like this when we were little, 'cause if so I don't remember it. I didn't know the South could *get* snow like this."

"Hmm? Oh sure, it happens once a decade or so," Mama said distractedly. "Why, in fact, the year Becca—"

Becca and I waited for her to go on, but she said nothing more. "The year Becca what?" I prodded.

"I don't remember anything like this *ever*." Becca's voice sounded small and little-girl-like from the backseat.

"Girls, really, I don't have time for this right now. Don't talk to me while I'm concentrating on the road. It's positively treacherous out here."

And it was. The Fairlane skidded once or twice on ice patches cleverly hidden by the snowfall, and I felt my heart lodge in my throat until the immediate danger passed and we were driving along again.

Back at the house Becca and I popped popcorn on the stove while Mama found a radio station playing Christmas carols. We danced around the living room to the jauntier tunes like "Sleigh Ride" and "Rudolph the Red-nosed Reindeer" then grew quiet when songs like "Silent Night" filled the room. Becca retrieved Mama's sewing box from down the hall and dug out two stout needles and thread for us to string the popcorn on. Mama stood near the living room window, digging through a box of ornaments, when she suddenly broke our dancing revelry. "Girls, are you expecting anyone tonight?"

Becca and I looked up, glancing first at one another and then shaking our heads in unison. "Why? Is someone—"

Mama's brow furrowed. "A car is turning in the driveway. Now I wonder who this could be. I'm not expecting Aunt Jess till Christmas Day, and I can't imagine who would brave the roads tonight." She took off her apron and reached the front door just as our mystery visitor rang the doorbell.

A gust of arctic wind blew into the living room as Mama opened the door, but no one was there. Whoever had rung the doorbell had obviously not wanted to be seen and in fact was backing hastily out of the driveway. But they had left something on the doorstep—a brown cardboard box tied with a red ribbon. Mama pushed the box inside with her foot and shoved the door closed against the cold.

"Did you get a look at the car?" I asked. Mama shook her head. We all stared down at the brown parcel, expecting it to be Aunt Jess's annual fruitcake come early, I suppose. What none of us expected was what it turned out to be—an anonymous gift for Becca that was too exquisite to be from a common local boy.

"Becca, it has your name on it," Mama said, peering at the brown cardboard with her reading glasses. Becca sank to the floor and pulled the midsize box into her lap, glancing up at us before slicing the taped edge with her fingernail. Inside was another box, this one wrapped in Christmas paper.

"Well, go on—unless you want to wait till Christmas morning," Mama said. "It's your choice, of course."

Becca stood abruptly, her eyes shining. "No, I want to open it alone, in my room. It might be something really special."

"Becca, have you been stringing another poor boy along? I do wish you would control your flirting." Mama tried to keep the annoyance out of her voice, but we both heard it.

The look of excitement in Becca's eyes was quickly shuttered, replaced by resentment. "What's it to you even if I am? Can't a girl have any privacy in this place? Look at you two—you're like vultures." She stalked down the hall, hugging her gift close, and slammed the door to our bedroom.

Mama tried to brush it off. "Gracious, what's gotten into her? Sometimes that girl is too high and mighty for her own good."

"It *was* her gift, Mama." *Defending her again.* "She didn't have to open it in front of us. Maybe it's something private . . . something special. Even though we're a family, that doesn't mean we're not individuals too, you know." The force of my words shocked me, but it was too late to take them back. They hung in the air between us, turning our festive night suddenly awkward.

"Yes, we are a family," Mama said in an odd tone,

and sighing. "I try. The Lord knows I try." She tied her apron back over her slender torso and disappeared into the kitchen, leaving me with the strains of "Ave Maria" coming from the radio and an undecorated tree standing forlorn in the living room. An hour passed, then two before I decided enough was enough. Surely Becca didn't need to hide away with her special gift this long, whatever it was. After winding the last of the twinkling lights on the tree and hanging all the ornaments myself, I went down the hall and tapped on our bedroom door.

"Who is it?" Becca called out. *As if she doesn't know.*

"It's me, can I come in?"

Instead of answering she scuffled to the door in her bedroom slippers and opened it a crack, giving me a blank stare.

"Well, what is it?"

Becca put her finger to her lips and motioned me into the room. Not thinking, I left the door partly open as I followed her to her matching twin bed and sat cross-legged, waiting for her to unveil the mysterious gift. Becca reached under her bed and pulled out an exquisite music box carousel, the kind we'd both seen in the most expensive store in Gideon. I knew it had cost someone a lot of money. Without a word she wound it up, and we watched wide-eyed as the carousel came to life. Tiny elephants, giraffes, zebras, and other exotic animals went up and down on their miniature carousel poles; a nutcracker prince danced round and round in circles with a ballerina princess, her stiff pink tutu made of real tulle.

"Oh my gosh, Becca! Do you have any idea who it's from?" I looked at her and saw her eyes flicker, already guessing her answer.

"I think I do." A wisp of a smile on her face.

A rustling sound at the door made us both turn our heads. Mama stood there, the same look of disapproval on her face. She muttered something about "too expensive" before shutting the door and padding down the hallway.

The next day, Christmas Eve, Becca and I trudged through the snow to the old Radcliffe place to escape the boredom of our snowbound house. Inside the creaking old house I quizzed my sister about her covert trips to the woodland cottage, and then again on the walk back home, wanting to make her feel a little guilty for leaving me out of her adventures.

She stopped suddenly and turned to face me, her eyes flaring. "Claire, don't you get it? You have Mama—you both have each other. It was just nice to have someone of my very own for once."

"What on earth are you talking about, Becca? What do you mean 'Mama and I have each other'? You've always been right there in the middle of everything."

"Oh Claire, don't be so dense," she shot back. "You know you've always been Mama's favorite, and sometimes I feel like I'm interrupting when I come upon the two of you laughing together or whatever."

Now I was thoroughly shocked at her words. Filtered through my childish memory, it had always seemed that Becca was the darling, the cute one, the daughter everybody gravitated to, the one who shone the brightest. Seeing my dumbfounded look, she went on.

"Gretchen was someone I didn't have to share, a secret friend, sort of, but I decided I would share her with you at Thanksgiving since we're leaving and all." She tossed a blonde ringlet out of her eye and walked faster. I saw her blink back tears. "I wanted to include you because you're my . . . my . . ."

"Your skizzer?" I offered, linking my arm through hers in that old way we had adopted long ago.

She laughed and sniffed loudly. "Yes, my skizzer."

We walked along in silence for a few minutes until Becca spoke again. "I mean, Mama is there for me and all, but . . . I don't know. Something's different about the way she treats me."

I started to refute her when suddenly a scene from our childhood skidded across my mind. Christmas morning, mounds of presents under the tree. Mama laughing as she watched Becca and me tear into our gifts and show them off. I clambered up onto the sofa, snuggling against Mama's soft breast, instinctively reaching my arm to include Becca in our group cuddle. But my sister hung back, eyeing our mother with an odd mixture of wariness and yearning until Mama patted the cushion on her other side and Becca joined in. Another scene: that day in the grocery store when Becca and I raced around a corner and knocked over a pyramid display of canned soup. Becca took the brunt of Mama's anger, even though I told her we both did the damage. She yelled at Becca right there in the store—out of character for Mama and causing a scene, as if the toppled display weren't enough humiliation. Other snippets of memory flitted through my mind, and I realized with that odd clarity that grips you every now and then just what Becca was talking about. And to think that, until this moment, I had never known. Never known it was she who felt inferior to me.

Looking back now, I know I truly learned something new about my sister that day—saw a facet of her character she had kept tightly shut up from everyone: namely, that outward ebullience can hide a depth of pain and insecurity. I think my growing up took a quantum leap because of it.

Two weeks later we packed up the car and followed the moving van south to Florida. Mama honked as we drove out of the neighborhood, past the low stone wall, past the old Radcliffe place—our way of saying good-bye.

"Say good-bye, girls!" she said cheerily as Becca and I looked out the windows, stone-faced and sullen. "Say good-bye!" Mama glanced over at me sitting in the front seat next to her. She reached out and squeezed my hand. "Everything's going to be all right, you'll see." Her words didn't seem to include Becca, who was sitting among a heap of boxes in the backseat.

I turned to glance at Becca, and she gave me a look that said, *Do you see what I mean?*

And I did see. I did see.

15

Gideon, North Carolina
June 2001

Standing before the lion's-head doorbell, waiting for Aunt Jess to answer the door, I told Rainey briefly what I'd learned at the library the night before.

He looked puzzled. "I don't get it."

We could both hear Aunt Jess approaching the door from the inside. "Did Becca ever tell you the story about the old woman named Gretchen? The old woman in the woods?"

His blank stare gave me my answer just as the heavy walnut door swung open. Aunt Jess smiled and extended her cheek for my kiss.

"There you are again, come in, come in. I've had Roberta prepare finger sandwiches for us. I thought we might visit on the back porch this time. The weather's been so nice lately. Hello, Ronald, it's good to see you again. Come on, you two, right this way."

I shot a grin at Rainey as we followed her through the

creaking old townhouse to the back porch. He rolled his eyes and grinned back. "Have you made any headway with your living estate sale, Aunt Jess?"

She mumbled something irritably and said the boy she'd hired to carry things down from the attic got sick with the flu, and now she either had to wait it out or find some new help. Passing through the rooms of her townhouse, I smelled the scent I would always equate with Aunt Jess—the cloying smell of mothballs. Still, there was a comforting nuance about the old place—the uneven hardwood floors, the windows with their original wavy-glass panes.

Out on the back porch, we nibbled the sandwiches and chatted. After a while I steered the conversation toward our real purpose for coming there again.

"Aunt Jess, remember the other day when I told you Becca was missing? Well, she's been gone over a week now, and the only reason I know she passed through North Carolina is because of the note she left me in our sister secret box."

"Your what?" Aunt Jess set her teacup back in the saucer and peered at me over her reading glasses. I told her about Becca leaving one day, how I found the note in the box buried where we played as children, and the letters from England that Rainey had discovered in her lingerie drawer, underneath the ruby crescent moon pendant. At the mention of the jewelry my aunt looked down and smoothed the linen napkin in her lap.

"I know you know something about the pendant, Aunt

Jess," I said. "And in fact I've been busy doing some digging myself—seems the past has more secrets than I realized." Rainey sat silent while I chose my next words. "A local jeweler told me the jewelry is rare and quite valuable. I know it's also linked to our family through the Lockwood line. Ever since Rainey told me he found the pendant in Becca's things I've had this nagging sense that it's somehow related to her disappearance."

I waited for a minute before I dropped my bombshell. "I also discovered at the library that my grandmother's full name was Dorothea Gretchen Trowling." Aunt Jess lifted her cropped gray head and studied me a long moment, waiting for me to continue. "Aunt Jess, did I ever tell you the story of what Becca and I found in the woods one summer when we were girls?"

She pinned me with her gaze. "You did not. Go on."

"A boy we hung out with in the neighborhood told us he had a surprise for us, some secret he'd found in the woods. The three of us set off one morning, and he led us to a cottage inhabited by an old woman named Gretchen. We visited with her, and Becca really took to the old lady. I'm sure Becca snuck back out to the woods to visit her now and then, and I'm pretty sure she's the one who gave Becca the crescent moon jewelry."

As I talked my aunt's face grew more serious until her eyes filled with a deep sadness. I set my hors d'oeuvres plate down and took her frail, blue-veined hand in mine. "Aunt Jess, whatever it is you're not telling me, I need to know."

She sighed and nodded. "It's time, I suppose. Old bones won't stay buried no matter how hard you try to cover them up with time and distance. But not here—if I'm going to tell you I want to tell you out there." She released her hand from mine, sat back in her chair, and nodded her head toward the western sky.

Rainey shot me a puzzled glance; we both waited.

"Did your mother ever take you to the ruins of the house where your grandfather and I were born?"

A cat yowled off in the distance. I waited for a moment before answering my aunt. "No, she mentioned it a few times but told Becca and me it burned to the ground long before we were born."

Aunt Jess paused while the housekeeper cleared the dishes away, and fixed her eyes on the abandoned goldfish pond in the townhouse's small, enclosed backyard. She had written a few years back that she was having a goldfish pond dug and lined with cement. She seemed so excited at the time, but something obviously went wrong, the fish now gone. All that remained was an oblong orifice in the ground filled with brackish water. The summer wind had picked up while we sat talking on the porch, and streaks of gray occluded the pale blue sky.

"If I tell you what you came to hear," Aunt Jess continued, clearing her throat, "it should be there, so you can get the look and feel of the place as the proper backdrop." She looked at Rainey. "Are you up for a little drive?"

"Wherever you ladies need to go."

As we left the town of Gideon behind and headed

east down a county road, suburban subdivisions gave way to rolling pastureland dotted with mobile homes. Occasionally a gas station that looked like it belonged to half a century earlier loomed up from the red earth, some with signs of humanity about them, others completely abandoned.

Rainey almost missed the turnoff, the road poorly marked amid a thatch of trees. After a quarter mile the asphalt grew rough in patches and the trees overhung the road, as if crowding close to watch our passage. Suddenly a clearing sprang into view, and I saw the ruins of the Meriwether estate.

Aunt Jess gestured from the front passenger seat. "Here we are. What is it, Claire? You look positively dumbstruck."

"I didn't realize so much of the house was still standing. I can't believe Mama never brought us here . . ."

"Well, good. At least once, I see, she followed my advice. What possible benefit could come from your visiting the site of all that tragic family history? Better to grow up blissfully ignorant than be drawn to a place that holds so much sadness."

I would never understand her generation's penchant for hiding skeletons in a closet, shielding children from the stories that made them, in part, who they were.

Rainey pulled the car under a sweet gum tree and cut the engine. We piled out of the car and looked around at this place steeped in history. In the foreground a series of stone steps had been cut into the earth, leading up to what once must have been a large portico. Leafy kudzu vines entwined one column's rotting upper half. The main part of the house with its ornate façade stood eerily silent amid the overgrowth. In the wing that had burned to the ground, three chimneys thrust up toward the sky as if in defiance of the calamity that betook the great house. I glanced at a massive tree on the far side of the house and had a sudden flashback—it was the same tree in the sepia photograph Gretchen gave to Becca, with a young version of herself standing beside a tire swing.

Aunt Jess led us to a low stone slab that might have been part of a fountain ledge in the house's heyday. Rainey placed the thick comforter he had brought along for my aunt on the slab. As she settled I passed her a thermos of apple juice and waited for her to begin. Aunt Jess sipped the liquid and gazed at the ruins of her childhood home.

"Picture a young man brought up to work hard with both his mind and his hands, making real estate investments and tilling the soil along with the people hired to do the work for him. That was your grandfather, Claire. Although his family had already made a fortune in tobacco by the mid-nineteenth century, Morgan Meriwether Trowling believed in the old way of doing things—learning from the ground up. He was your great-grandparents' only son, the only male to carry on the family name, and he was a fine specimen in every way. One daughter came along in due time—me—but among the landed gentry daughters are not as important as sons because everyone knows daughters marry and take on a new name.

"By the time Morgan was twenty-eight, he was running the estate and the family business interests. Our own father had too high a regard for whiskey, and it had started to show. Mother was only too happy to let her tall, impressive son represent the family in both society and business dealings. I was twenty-one by the time Morgan confided in me that he was ready to take a wife. Oh, he had choices aplenty, you can be sure of that. Every marriageable young woman in the tri-county area had set her cap for my brother. He was handsome, with a crop of thick, curly hair, and of course he was rich as Laban. But Morgan was about the pickiest man I ever saw. Mother made sure he attended the most important debutante balls, but he always came home and pronounced the local girls a tiresome bore.

"One day he drove over to Charlotte to meet with a business associate—someone I'd never heard him mention before. Well, he kept going back to Charlotte, and eventually he met a girl there and fell hard for her. He was absolutely besotted. In the early mornings, long before the house stirred, you could hear Morgan singing like a lovesick puppy as he walked the tobacco fields near our home. He had a beautiful singing voice, did I mention, and now that he was in love—well, I guess you could say his heart was stirred to music. The sound of his singing carried on the wind all the way back to the house, and I couldn't stay asleep long once I heard it.

"This young woman was named Dorothea Sanderson, and Morgan said he met her at the theater one night in Charlotte. Naturally we all thought he meant *at* the theater, the acquaintance of his business associate perhaps, but years later he told me Dorothea was an actress, and the moment he saw her onstage he vowed to have her. He kept this choice bit of information from my mother and me for some time, as I said. Father was too tipsy half the time to care. I think Morgan knew Mother would consider a local stage actress too common for her son, and so he kept his own counsel about the matter until the wedding was past and a few years had worn the sheen off the marriage."

Aunt Jess shifted on the stone slab and set the thermos aside. With both hands free, she clutched her cardigan around her shoulders and hunched forward against the wind. She resembled a gray-headed toddler with her small head poking out through the bulky fabric.

"Dorothea was enchanting at first and very beautiful," she continued. "Soon the whole household was smitten with her charms. All except me. I've always been blessed with a certain cynicism, you could say—or maybe it's a keen sense of judgment when it comes to people. At any rate, there was something about Dorothea that just didn't add up for me. But I treated her cordially, and she and Morgan moved into the rooms he added onto the house for their private quarters. A year passed, and one day Dorothea announced she was carrying a child. After a difficult confinement she delivered a healthy, pink baby girl—this would be your mother, Claire. Constance was a delightful baby, and she brought laughter back into the house. Mother doted on her and almost never left her side. Meanwhile, the baby's own mother gradually slipped into a deep depression. The postpartum malady, I realize now, perhaps complicated by her own tendency toward melancholy, but whatever the reason she lost all interest in being a mother.

"My own mother, your great-grandmother, hired a nursemaid to care for the baby. Dorothea began to feel like a prisoner in her husband's house—the house she would run one day as Mistress Trowling. She started taking long walks alone in the woods surrounding the estate. When Morgan told her it wasn't seemly for a gentlewoman to wander the woods alone, she threw a screaming tantrum and shut herself into her chamber and refused to eat for a week.

"Morgan always put Dorothea on a pedestal, and he doted on her, but by now Mother really despised the girl—she was so far beneath her original expectations for Morgan, beautiful though she was. Mother also had me to worry about. I had never been one to fancy boys much. She traipsed me around to all the society balls, but I was never a great beauty, you understand, and I was so strong-minded and independent I think I scared the young men half to death.

"And so as the years ticked by and still no suitor emerged to claim me, I found a purpose in helping Morgan run the family business. To everyone's surprise, I had quite a head for it, and Morgan turned over the bookkeeping to me. I would disappear into the office for hours on end, content to hole up with the books and ledgers that kept the Trowling estate rolling along in the black.

"Dorothea, on the other hand, missed the stage so badly she started performing little one-act skits that we were all obliged to watch. Morgan's face would light up as he watched her perform, but I always thought her acting a bit overdone—too melodramatic, with all that arm flailing and gliding about. Her odd spells grew more frequent. One night during an important dinner party she grew so agitated when a guest nervously tapped the table with his fingers that she clapped her hands over her ears and shrieked for him to stop. Morgan was afraid to let her attend important social functions after that, and he started making excuses for her. Mrs. Trowling has a headache, Mrs. Trowling is indisposed at the moment, Mrs. Trowling is out of town visiting relatives.

"The year your mother turned three, everything came to a head. Toddlers are very demanding, and Dorothea simply couldn't cope. She was putting the finishing touches on a skit she expected to perform for the family and household servants on the Fourth of July. Looking back, it's hard to believe she got in a tizzy over such a trifling affair, but she was wound up as tight as a drum. She would pace the upstairs hallways, reciting her lines and driving the servants crazy with her posturing. When her lines didn't come out the way she wanted, or someone expressed the slightest disinterest, Dorothea would sink into a depression and lock herself in her room on a crying jag. Or she would sneak out on one of her woodland walks.

"Three days before the big event Dorothea announced that she needed to go to Charlotte to borrow a few props from her old theater. Morgan didn't want her to go, but she got her way in the end, driving herself to Charlotte. My brother worried himself to distraction; Mother said maybe the short time away would help settle his wife's nerves and she would return home her old self.

"The morning of the Fourth arrived, and around eleven o'clock Dorothea's car turned into the drive on schedule. Morgan, who had been watching for her from the library balcony, ran down to greet his wife at the front door. Dorothea stepped through the door with a peculiar serenity about her, and she held her head a little higher, I thought, like a queen returned to her rightful home. Something about her was changed; I knew it at once. Women often do, you know. But of course, all Morgan saw was his lovely bride, back in her right mind as Mother had predicted.

"That evening, after attending the fireworks display in downtown Gideon, the family all gathered to watch Dorothea's Elizabethan skit. We applauded her heartily. As she took her bows I saw something shiny spill out of her bodice. In the second before she tucked it back into her neckline, I recognized the family heirloom pendant—a gold crescent moon with an inset ruby eye.

It was an heirloom that was passed to a favored wife or daughter of each generation, but Mother had refused to relinquish the jewelry to Dorothea, considering her unworthy. I think she was waiting to see if the marriage survived beyond just a few years.

"I said nothing but determined to check Mother's jewelry box the next day to make sure the heirloom was returned. I never got a chance. By noon on July fifth, Dorothea still hadn't emerged from her chamber. We all knew she liked to sleep late, so no one was too alarmed. Morgan confided to me that he had tried to enter his wife's room the night before, wanting to celebrate her stage performance, but she had complained of a headache and overwrought nerves.

"Betsy, our cook, prepared a light breakfast to be sent to Dorothea's room. The upstairs maid had taken the day off, so Betsy had to find someone else to carry the tray. When she called in the parlormaid, the girl looked at her oddly, as if her request made no sense. Betsy pressed her, and the girl said she'd seen Dorothea creep out of the house just before dawn with a carpetbag, heading across the tobacco fields toward the woods."

Aunt Jess paused in her story and sat silent for a few moments. Unexpectedly, she rose from the stone slab and asked Rainey and me to follow her. Without another word, she led us to the eastern side of the property, through low bracken and a border of trees about half a block thick. We emerged into a clearing that spilled onto a large tobacco field. Long ago someone had cut a path along the perimeter of the crop field on all four sides. Here where we stood, facing east, the path led about three football field lengths to a dense forest, where the path took an abrupt left turn onto the northern side of the field. If one continued forward where the path turned north, all that lay before them was woods.

Aunt Jess lifted her cane and pointed at the woods. "There, that's the direction the parlormaid said your grandmother headed on the morning of July 5, 1952. Most likely her curiosity got the best of her, and she followed Dorothea at a distance for a little ways. Otherwise she couldn't have seen this far from the house."

My mind was already whirling and drawing conclusions, but something didn't add up. Just as I was about to ask a question Aunt Jess turned and headed back toward the ruins. "Morgan searched the woods tirelessly, of course," she called back over her shoulder as we followed. "Even sent out a search party. I, on the other hand, carried out a secret plot that I've never confessed to another living soul."

Back at the stone slab, Aunt Jess perched on the edge to finish her story. "When I heard the direction Dorothea headed that morning, I knew immediately where she would go. You see, it so happens that on a previous occasion when Dorothea took one of her walks in the woods, I had been seated in my favorite reading spot—the broad horseback limb of a willow tree that stands just inside the woods at the edge of the tobacco field. Years earlier, when Morgan discovered I loved to read there as a child, he nailed wooden slats into the massive trunk so I could climb up into the tree's heights without a struggle. I was reading *Moby Dick*—I remember it distinctly—when the sound of a woman's skirts whooshed by below. It was Dorothea. I let her get far enough ahead not to notice me, and then I followed her deep into the woods until she arrived at a small clearing that contained an abandoned caretaker's cottage.

"I watched for a while, but when Dorothea disappeared inside the cottage and stayed there, I finally got bored and turned back for home. I figured she had claimed the spot as her private refuge, and who was I to deny her that? Another time I saw her head into the woods carrying a small parcel. I believe that little by little she made that cottage livable—or at least comfortable enough for an afternoon's respite.

"Two days passed and still the men weren't able to find Dorothea. Morgan began to fear the worst, but I gave him false hope, telling him I was sure she would turn up in due time." Aunt Jess paused, and when I glanced at her I saw her eyes glistening. She was not a sentimental woman, so I knew that whatever came next in her story must have troubled her for a long time.

"After the search parties ceased, people started whispering that Dorothea had managed to escape back to Charlotte. Others claimed she took her own life, but a body never turned up. I had my own ideas about her disappearance, as I've already intimated, and so one day after the kafuffle had settled down a bit I pretended I was going to the willow tree to read. Of course I headed straight to the cottage, and there was Dorothea. You may be wondering how a party of strong men had missed the cottage altogether. Let me explain. The cottage was located on the far side of a ravine that could only be traversed by clawing one's way down into the gash of red earth that split the forest in two. It was messy work, as I'd found out the day I first followed Dorothea to the cottage. No doubt the men deemed it impassable for a woman as delicate as she, but they didn't know Dorothea was reared on a farm and roamed the countryside as a girl.

"I knocked on the door of the cottage, but I needn't have bothered. Dorothea had already spotted me through the window. I don't know if her instinct told her I would be her ally or not—she knew I didn't like her and probably guessed I was only too happy to be rid of her—but for whatever reason she opened the door and let me in.

"As it turned out, my own instincts about your grandmother were right. You recall how I'd sensed a change in her that morning when she looked like she hid a delightful secret. Well, she carried a secret all right—right in her belly. Dorothea told me she believed she was pregnant, one of those uncanny hunches women get. Not with Morgan's child, you understand, but a love child from a man back in Charlotte whom she'd loved since childhood. He wasn't wealthy, and so she set her cap for my brother instead, but apparently old flames die hard. The ruse about needing props for her skit was just that, a ruse. She stayed with this man for the next two days—certainly long enough to get in the family way. But, alas, it was the wrong family, and Dorothea knew Morgan would discover her sin. She hadn't let him near her bedroom for months."

Dusk crept along the sky, so Rainey suggested we leave the ruins and head back to Aunt Jess's townhouse. I turned for one last look at my family's ruined estate. The charred stones and the wind in the trees whispered of an era stranger than I had expected. No wonder my mother had never wanted to return here.

As we bumped along on the drive back to Aunt Jess's townhouse, the county road that led into town held much more interest for me than it had on our trip out here. Now the countryside surrounding the thin strip of fading asphalt leapt to life with the names, faces, and events of the story I had just heard. I shook my head, still astounded that I'd been allowed to grow up with the ruins of my family's estate less than ten miles away.

16

Gideon, North Carolina
June 2001

Back at the townhouse, Aunt Jess led us to her living room and continued her story. "I told Dorothea I would help her get back to Charlotte and start a new life, away from my brother. Instead, she asked for my assistance in living a life hidden away from society, somewhere she could raise her child alone. She was tired, she said. Tired of everything and everyone. I found an apartment with a discreet landlady in a small town about forty miles away. Dorothea set up house there. In due time the baby came, and it was another little girl. She named her Lily, and this baby she adored—the love child, you know. By now I was keeping all the estate books, and so I saw to it that Dorothea and Lily were taken care of. That was my part of the bargain. Her part was to keep away and never come back.

"As you can imagine, the household was in turmoil

all this time. Morgan couldn't accept the fact that his wife had left him."

I glanced at Rainey; he looked uneasy and wouldn't meet my eyes. Without a word I hooked my arm through his for reassurance.

"Morgan cancelled all his business appointments and kept searching for Dorothea," Aunt Jess continued, her voice a monotone now. "This next part is difficult for me to tell you, but if you're going to hear the story you might as well hear all of it. It broke my heart to see my beloved brother so torn up over an undeserving woman—at least, that's how I saw things then. I decided something needed to be done. Morgan needed closure. A person with money always has access to . . . exceptional resources. I used the Trowling money and my connections to procure suitable remains that would close the case on Dorothea Trowling, nee Sanderson. I hired a man to bury the remains half hidden from view, but visible enough so that a search party found them—found her, or so they thought. You have to remember this was long before forensic science could identify human remains through DNA testing. The coroner was satisfied, the search party was satisfied, and ultimately even my distraught brother came to terms with the fact that his beautiful bride had wandered into the woods and died.

"Their marriage lasted only four years, but in that short time I watched my brother transform from a robust, visionary man to a distraught, tormented soul—all because of a romantic nature he inherited from our father. Morgan was better off believing her to be dead. Or so I told myself."

Aunt Jess's voice broke off, and she looked down at her hands in her lap. "Another year passed, and by then my brother was a changed man. He took to the bottle like his father before him. I would smell whiskey on his breath at the breakfast table, for Pete's sake. On the Fourth of July, one year since the trouble began, he gave all the household servants the day off. He even shooed Mother and me out of the house, urging us to spend the day in town. But we played along. Apparently Morgan needed a day to himself, I reasoned, and I was only too eager to help him in any way I could."

A bird swooped out of a tree outside, screeching as it dipped and rose again, heading west on its ascent. My eyes followed it as Aunt Jess finished her story.

"The town of Gideon was in full swing for the Independence Day celebration. Everywhere people were setting off firecrackers and lighting sparklers. The whole town smelled like smoke, so none of us saw it coming. The first sign of trouble was a thin, gray ribbon of smoke curling up into the sky west of town. Soon it looked like an atom bomb had exploded, and it lay in the direction of home. Mother and I overheard an agitated woman on the sidewalk talking loudly about a fire, and I think we both knew then. The fire truck siren screamed as the truck careened down Main Street. I drove us back to our home, or what was left of it.

"I'll never forget the sight of my beloved home engulfed in flames and black smoke as we rounded the last curve of the long driveway. How surreal it all was, like a disturbing movie in slow motion. Later, the sheriff's office determined that Morgan set the house on fire and then shot himself in the library. The fire was beyond control by the time the firemen got there. Mother ran to check on the few farm animals we kept, but I just stood there and cried. Yes, I bawled like a baby—for Morgan, for my beautiful home, for the sadness that had engulfed all of us those past few years."

Rainey and I sat stunned, almost afraid to breathe in the silence. When at last I ventured to speak, my voice came out barely above a whisper.

"What did you all do, Aunt Jess? Where did you go?"

For the first time in her long soliloquy my aunt turned and looked me in the eye, but it was not the bold eagle-eyed stare so characteristic of her. In her eyes I saw a deep sadness coupled with something else. Defeat.

"We were all scattered to the four winds," she said after a moment, "those of us who survived long enough to tell of it. Mother and Father moved into a bungalow they owned on the outskirts of town, avoiding social gatherings. Father died within the year of a heart attack, and Mother followed a year later. A stroke, or so the doctor said. I believe she died of a broken heart. The servants were all let go, and I settled in town. But the story doesn't end there. You see, I had little Constance—your mother—to care for now that both her parents were gone. Her nanny and I raised that girl into a fine young woman. She didn't marry well, of course—went against my wishes in that regard. But I always felt a burden to give her extra special care because I knew she was the cast-off one, the child Dorothea didn't give two pence for. Tragic. It's no wonder she chose a ne'er-do-well for a husband, who also abandoned her. Besides the nanny and me, that's what everyone else did to her. It was the only pattern she knew."

A vivid new picture of my mother sprang to mind. I had always thought of her as quiet yet capable, a hearth-and-home sort of woman blessed with a strong nature. Yet I had to admit she had few women friends when we were growing up. She volunteered for everything and made sure we never missed a church service, but I couldn't recall a single time she invited a friend over "just to visit." People smiled and nodded at our little female family whenever we went into town to shop, but rarely did someone actually stop to chat. It had never occurred to me that, like Becca, Mama might have held people at arm's length—a way of rejecting them before they rejected her.

Aunt Jess continued. "Meanwhile, when Lily grew to school age, I made arrangements for her to attend a good private school. A housekeeper-nanny also made sure that young lady got a decent upbringing, as I wasn't sure how long Dorothea's warmth toward the child would last. The truth is, I think Dorothea thrived in the quiet, reclusive life she chose. There were no demands on her, you see. No expectations. Nobody pulling at her from all sides.

"But history often repeats itself, as they say. When Lily was sixteen, she got pregnant by a local boy and ran off with him. She left the baby wrapped in the bassinet with a note pinned to the side, and nobody ever heard from her again. Dorothea made the only trip I knew her to take to bring the baby to me. She didn't want to raise another generation, she said, and the nanny had left a few years earlier when Lily was old enough not to need one. By this time, your mother was a young married woman with a child of her own—you, Claire. I brought Lily's baby to her and asked if she would raise the infant as her own daughter. I never told her who the baby really was, but I believe she suspected that she was a blood relation somehow. She took the child and named her Rebecca Ruth. That little girl grew up as your sister, Becca."

I could feel my eyes grow large. "Aunt Jess, do you mean to tell me that Becca is really my cousin?"

"I'm afraid so, dear." The clock on the mantelpiece ticked out the seconds, ignoring the weight of the words she had just delivered. They felt heavy and ponderous in my ears, and I struggled to process what my aunt had just said.

"But does it really matter?" Aunt Jess prodded. "Flesh and blood is still flesh and blood, and she was raised as your sister. I hope it doesn't change how you feel about Becca."

I stood up and paced the creaky floorboards, my mind whirling with thoughts, flashes of memory, questions, and suppositions all at once. I was numb and suddenly mute, needing time to think about what I'd just heard. Without a word to either of them, I stepped out the back door and stared at Aunt Jess's abandoned goldfish pond. Maybe an hour passed while I stared at the stagnant water, or maybe it was fifteen minutes—I lost track as my mind tumbled over memories from our childhood. *She knew*, I suddenly realized. *Becca knew all along that she was different—that she somehow didn't "belong" to our little family.* What was it she had said the day of our farewell tea party with Gretchen—our grandmother, I now realized? *"Mama is there for me and all, but . . . something's different about the way she treats me."*

A hand touched my shoulder, hesitant yet comforting. It was Rainey, a pained look in his eyes again. I saw the unspoken question in their depths. "What are you expecting me to say, Rain? That I don't care for Becca anymore now that I've learned her true parentage? That I've suddenly grown cold and unfeeling and don't care whether she ever comes home? Of course I still feel the same about Becca. She's . . . she's my sister. She always will be as far as I'm concerned. I just need a little time to take all this in. I've just had a bomb dropped on me."

"Yes," Aunt Jess interjected from the back porch, "but you asked me to tell you what I knew and so I did. Sooner or later you would have learned the truth anyway."

I stared at her dumbfounded and stepped back onto the porch. "When were you going to tell me? It's not like I'm twelve years old, Aunt Jess. Or did you plan to bury this one with you?"

Aunt Jess remained calm. "I was waiting for the proper time. It's true, perhaps I waited too long, and I'm not sure when the right time would have come. Maybe I prolonged the difficult and it was easier to just let the years go by without any unpleasantness. There was so much of that, you see, in earlier years. Despite the departure of your father—I doubt you even remember him, you were so young—you and Becca had a happy childhood, and your mother poured on you two little girls all the love she never got in her own unhappy youth.

"And so that's the whole story," she said, exhaling deeply, "all except one little item. Although I continued to send money to Dorothea every month, some years later she wrote and asked me to start sending the checks to a P.O. box in Gideon under a different name. I thought it odd at the time, but I obliged her. Later still I heard rumors of a strange old woman who came into town once a month to stock up on groceries and then disappeared again. The local children made up fantastic stories about her."

Aunt Jess fixed me with her sharp gaze. "But this is the interesting part, Claire. Not until you told me the story about the old woman in the woods did I realize she must have moved back to that cottage of hers. And the name she asked me to inscribe on her checks was Gretchen Sanderson. Dorothea Gretchen Sanderson—that was your grandmother's given name."

"Aunt Jess, is my grandmother even still alive?"

She nodded. "Oh yes. As recent as last month she cashed the check I send her every four weeks. I think you and Ronald stand a very good chance of finding Dorothea still kicking. For now I'm tired, Claire. I hope you won't begrudge an old woman her afternoon nap."

I helped her to her bedroom. As we made our way up the creaking stairs of the townhouse, one last question popped into my mind. I settled Aunt Jess in her bed and tucked the coverlet around her before venturing to ask.

"Aunt Jess, just one more thing and then I promise I'll go—pinkie promise." I held out my little finger, waiting for her response.

Her blue eyes flickered open and she smiled, a rare moment when she let her softer side show through. "You always were a persistent little bugger, Claire. Pinkie promise accepted. Now ask your question and be done with it."

"You never told us what happened to the family heirloom, the crescent moon pendant you suspected my grandmother of taking. Obviously it was in her possession if she was able to bequeath it to Becca."

"Ah yes, so I didn't." Aunt Jess nodded. "Indeed Dorothea did take it—and took good care of it, by all accounts.

After I had seen her settled into the apartment when she was pregnant with Lily, I asked her to return the jewelry, as Mother never intended her to have it. She refused, said she wanted to save it for her Lily someday. I don't easily take no for an answer, but she pulled out the big guns. Blackmail. If I wrested the heirloom from her, she said, she would blow the whistle on my cover-up scheme and reveal the measures I had taken to contrive her fictitious death. Dorothea could be feisty when she wanted something badly enough. To this day I believe she affected all that eccentricity of hers. She was an actress, remember."

I smiled in spite of myself. "And so when Lily ran off as a teenager, I suppose my grandmother decided to give the heirloom to Becca instead. Once she was old enough, that is."

"Yes, I suppose so." Aunt Jess closed her eyes again and sighed wearily. "And that's where the story passes to your sister and you."

I pushed the gas pedal harder than I intended, speeding away from my aunt's townhouse back toward the hotel. I was both troubled and stirred at what she had just told me. Meanwhile, Rainey was trying to figure out the best turnoff point from the county road into the woods. I didn't want to discourage him, but I thought of how much a forest can change over the course of several decades. Yet he was a man on a mission. He would find the cottage—and my grandmother if she was still alive—and hopefully find clues to Becca's whereabouts. We planned to make a pit stop at the hotel, change into rugged clothing, and then head out to find my grandmother's reclusive home in the forest while there was still daylight.

Rainey was quiet, giving me space for my thoughts—a gesture I appreciated. Dark rain clouds moved across the sky as we drove the last few miles to the hotel, and the distant rumble of thunder shook the afternoon sky. We both craned our necks and looked out the car windows at the impending thunderstorm.

"What do you think, Rain? Are you up to sluicing through mud, or shall we wait till tomorrow?"

His eyes probed the sky. "Are you kidding? I'm not about to let a little rain and lightning stop me now." Suddenly my brother-in-law looked at me, his eyes so pleading and hopeful it broke my heart. "Do you really think we stand a good chance of finding her there, Claire? I mean, you said she had a strange connection to Dorothea when you were girls—long before she could have known who the old lady was. You guys hiked out there on your own when you were kids, right?"

"Yes, Rainey, I do think we stand a good chance of finding Becca. She did plant a clue for me—for us—right here where we grew up, after all."

But what I didn't tell him was the feeling in my gut that Becca wasn't in North Carolina anymore, nor even in the country perhaps, but far across the Atlantic in a small English town.

17

Gideon, North Carolina
June 2001

I studied the crude map Aunt Jess made showing us where to park, about halfway between the Meriwether estate and downtown Gideon. We found the spot easily enough—a bit more overgrown than Aunt Jess may have recollected—but that served to our benefit. Rainey pulled the car behind an oversize clump of honeysuckle, and we put on our galoshes and ponchos.

By now the storm had faded to a steady drizzle, but the iron-gray sky diminished the daylight. It would be much harder to see once we entered the woods. Even on blinding summer days those woods were cool and dark in the deepest recesses, I remembered. But Rainey had apparently thought of that already; he retrieved a hefty flashlight from the trunk and looped it around his neck like a canteen. A machete, sheathed in its scabbard, dangled at his side. He looked like a safari scout ready for the bush.

I could read his excitement as he looked up at me. "Come on, let's go find my wife."

About seventy-five feet from the road the grassy ground took a sudden drop and gave way to forest. Someone had cut a well-trod path there. At first it was visible only by the flattened grass, but as we neared the woods the path took on more definite borders. I followed Rainey into the woods and glanced over my shoulder as we left the gloomy sunlight behind. The ground that lay ahead of us and on all sides loomed as dark as Snow White's forest, and I imagined eyes watched us too as the trees closed behind us, locking us into a world of sodden branches, gnarled roots, and low-hanging mist.

The rain struggled to penetrate the thick canopy of trees, but a steady drip-drip from the branches found its way onto our heads as we trudged along. Every now and then one of us slipped on the muddy path, but otherwise the walk was a lot easier than I'd expected. Fifteen minutes later, I had to eat my thoughts. When Rainey and I reached a massive fallen log, the path abruptly ended.

Rainey scrambled up onto the log and shone his flashlight into the dense woods beyond. Nothing. Not a trace of a footpath emerged, not even the overgrown remnants of one. Undaunted, he slid back down the rounded side of the trunk and explored the woods on either side of the path leading up to that point. I followed him tentatively but kept one eye trained on the footpath. I knew how dense and deep this forest was and remembered a story from childhood about two boys who ventured too far and never made it back—except in body bags.

We searched for another hour, trying to pick up the trail or find some sign of a detour a person familiar with the woods might use. As I explored the woods I thought of Becca and the remarkable discovery I'd made about her that day, courtesy of Aunt Jess. I'd blurted out that of course she was still a sister to me, that the news of our separate parentage didn't matter—or change anything. But did it? How does one swallow news like that in one gulp and keep going as if nothing's changed? Scenes from our childhood flittered across my mind—with her always in the role of little sister—and I wondered how I would act toward Becca when we did meet again.

Glancing at the darkening sky through the treetops, I decided it was time to call it a day.

"Rain, it's no good—this path might have been used by my grandmother a long time ago, or someone who helped her, but it can't be the way forward to the cottage now."

He wiped his sleeve across his brow to clear the rain from his eyes and nodded. "I know. I just kept hoping, but beyond this log the woods really are impassable. There's no way an old woman could make the trip. Heck, we can't even penetrate these woods beyond here."

I nodded, seeing his disappointment. "Remember I said the only way I ever reached the cottage was through the woods in our backyard? Well, that's what I think we need to do. I don't know who lives in our old house now, but I'm sure we can creep back there and find the trail if it still exists. Once we're on the trail I can probably get us there."

The next day I drove us out to the neighborhood where Becca and I grew up. Our old house looked recently lived in but deserted for now. With no signs of life lurking about, we decided to park the car in front as if we were a house-hunting couple inspecting a property. Rainey let me lead the way behind the house to the woods beyond. I found the old footpath without too much trouble—a bit overgrown but still visible; the neighborhood kids must be keeping it active—and we plunged into the dense green forest.

The woods had indeed changed over the decades that stretched behind me. Yet someone had obviously kept the path clear past leaf-clotted streams, across fallen deadwood, through glades and brambles, and finally beyond the red-clay ravine that I remembered so well from my childhood. After trekking nearly an hour, we came to a place where the footpath forked. Straight ahead or veer to the left? Rainey gazed at me, waiting for my lead.

"Your call, Davy Crockett. I'm just along for the ride until we get there. Do you remember a fork in the path?" He swatted a mosquito on his neck.

I studied the two paths and nodded. "Yes, if you can call it that. What I do remember is Joe Spivey crashing through the woods to the left of the path at some undefined point beyond the ravine."

He grinned. "Well, does this feel like the right undefined spot?"

Without a word I pushed through the bracken as Joe Spivey had done, taking the fork on the left. Now that he sensed we were close, I could hear Rainey's breath coming in short gasps, partly from exertion and partly from the adrenaline rush of knowing he might see Becca in a few minutes. I crashed headlong, small twigs and willowy, budding branches snapping back in my face as we plunged forward. I don't know how long this continued, but just when I thought I couldn't take any more of the stinging slaps and scrapes against my arms and face we emerged in a clearing. And there was my grandmother's cottage, only refurbished. Someone had even added a coat of paint in the last few years. We didn't waste any time but stepped up to the door and knocked.

The door opened to reveal an old woman I recognized at once. "Ah, so you've finally come. You are my granddaughter Claire, aren't you?"

"Grandmother—yes, it's me, Claire."

"Is my wife here?" Rainey blurted, then caught himself. "Excuse me, ma'am, but I'm looking for Becca, and we thought she might be here with you."

My grandmother opened the door wide, and we

stepped into the one-room cottage. She ignored Rainey's question for the time being. "My dear, turn around so I can get a look at you." Her ancient eyes glistened as she spoke, and I realized for the first time that I was gazing into the face of my own flesh and blood, the woman who had cast off my mother but then embraced the girl I grew up calling my sister. She seemed to study me as a specimen under a glass, soaking in the details to make up for lost time. I didn't know how to act toward this elderly relation, even if she was my grandmother. Two days ago my maternal grandmother was little more than a name in a dusty book, a hazy memory from my own mother's childhood, passed down to me in bits and snatches of Trowling lore—a person who presumably died in young womanhood and held no real bearing on my life today. But she did, I realized with a sudden clarity. This woman, Dorothea Gretchen Trowling, held the key to everything Rainey and I sought.

One glance around the tiny house told us both that Becca was not there. Perhaps she was returning soon though, or out collecting firewood, or whatever one did when she lived in the forest. I heard Rainey's sigh, the breathing out of yet one more hope. After scanning the room, my eyes settled back on my grandmother. She pointed us toward a small threadbare sofa and seated herself at the wooden table in the center of the room.

"I was wondering when you would get here."

My heart thudded in my chest. "So you knew I would come. Grandmother, why didn't you reveal yourself to Becca and me all those years ago? Why did you let us grow up not knowing you?" I waited for an answer, but she remained silent, as if pondering how to possibly answer such a question with mere words.

"You let us find you . . . here . . . and then go away again without ever knowing who you really were. Was it some kind of odd little game you played, a repeat of your dramatic flairs when you were younger? I could have benefited from knowing my grandmother all those years ago, despite whatever issues you had going on. So could Becca." My anger spilled out, more caustic than I'd intended. "Where is my sister, anyway? Has she been here?"

"Yes," she nodded, uttering the one word and then sitting silent again. Rainey and I exchanged glances. Outside the wind picked up, whining through the cracks in the wooden walls.

"But you're too late. Becca found what she was looking for and left over a week ago."

Rainey's voice was gentle as he spoke. I knew the restraint it must have taken him. "And what was she looking for that could make her disappear so suddenly, Mrs. Trowling? What could possibly be both terrible and wonderful enough for that?"

My grandmother returned his gaze steadily, her blue-veined hands folded in front of her on the sagging table. "Why, her own mother, my dear."

18

"Her mother?" The voice that spoke was my own. "So that means—"

"That Lily is alive after all these years, yes." She studied me with lively eyes, sizing up how much I knew. "So you've had a thorough visit with Jessica, I see. How much of the story did she tell you?"

"Everything—at least I hope so—and I have to say it sounded like a tale out of some weird Southern gothic novel. I never knew my family was so . . . colorful."

My grandmother smiled and nodded, still pinning me with those quizzical amber eyes; Becca's eyes, I suddenly realized. I shifted on the sofa. "Truth is always stranger than fiction, my dear, and any realist worth his salt must know that."

"Ma'am, Claire and I have spent the past several days looking for Becca," Rainey said. "I traveled eight hundred miles to get here. Can you tell me where she is—and why she came here in the first place?"

"It would be easier if I showed you. Claire, will you fetch that letter on my dressing table? It's there, in the corner nook."

I glanced in the direction she pointed and saw the antique miniature dressing table that had caught my attention when we came to the cottage as children. The same sepia photograph of a young woman sat in the precise spot I remembered it, as if my grandmother hadn't disturbed its place for more than two decades. A photo of herself, I now realized, wondering why I hadn't seen the likeness before. Indeed she had been beautiful once—and full of spit and vinegar as she said to Joe Spivey. A letter lay next to the framed photograph, but unlike the picture it looked to be contemporary. I took the letter to my grandmother and sat down at the table opposite her in the only other chair.

She unfolded the letter and handed it to Rainey, who had sprung up from the sofa and now sank to his knees on the floor next to me so we could read the letter together.

"This is the same stationery all those letters from England are written on," he said under his breath, turning the envelope over to be sure. Inside was a two-page letter written in an unfamiliar hand. Nothing at all like Becca's sloping script. Even before Rainey checked the closing on page two—which read "Your loving mother, Lily"—I knew who it was from.

The letter was dated six months ago. We read it together in silence while Dorothea watched. After introducing herself and filling in her background in Becca's life she wrote these words:

My little Rebecca, how I have longed to see you these past three decades, but the time was never right—I was never right—and so I left you to be reared by your grandmother. Only later did I discover you were in fact brought up by my half sister Constance, a woman I never knew. Dorothea assures me that you had a very happy childhood—with a sister to call your own—and have grown into a fine young woman. After I ran away with your father (believe me, he doesn't warrant the term "your father") I almost came back, but as the months turned into years, and the years passed into decades, I realized you were better off believing Constance was your mother. It could only cause you pain to learn that your real mother battled the twin demons of alcohol and manic-depression. I despised myself, so how could my tiny daughter possibly feel anything but revulsion for me? So goes the logic of one deemed unstable, unfit, by society, regardless of a pretty face. That at least I was able to pass down to you, as Dorothea assures me you are a beautiful woman both inside and out. Even if she only saw you from afar as you grew up, and she relied on yearly school photos to track your progress. (Yes, your Aunt Jessica was always dependable that way.) Until that extraordinary summer when you found her cottage in the woods and struck up a friendship. I only heard about this in the past year when I contacted Dorothea to tell her the news that compels me to seek you out at last. You see, I am dying and cannot leave this earth until I see your sweet face one more time.

Oh, Rebecca! I have so much to tell you—a lifetime to catch up on before I pass from this world. Perhaps you are angry at me for abandoning you as a baby. You have a right to be. If you do not wish to see me, I will understand. But if you can find it in your heart to forgive me, write me back at the address on the envelope. I've been staying in England with a friend (that's another story, for another time), but at one word from you I will make my way back to the States, Lord willing, so I can see you again and you can finally know . . .

Your loving mother,

Lily

P.S. I have something wonderful to share with you, but it's the kind of news best served up face-to-face, perhaps over a cup of English tea.

I glanced at Rainey's face and saw a mixture of relief and consternation on it. At last his fears about another man were dispelled, but in their place was what I could only guess to be a sense of betrayal. Why couldn't Becca share this part of her life with him? Why couldn't she draw him into her discovery of her birth mother? Why did she disappear without a warning—or at the very least a phone call later to assure Rainey she was safe and sound?

Instantly my mind supplied the answer: because she knew him too well. She knew that if Rainey discovered her whereabouts, he would jump the next plane to fetch her home. My intuitive sister needed this time alone with the mother she never knew. But her sense of loyalty and drama led her to leave a clue for me, knowing that by the time we found her she would have had her last meeting with Lily.

Dorothea (I had already resolved to call her this, her first name) rose from the table and stepped over to a small wood-burning stove. With the slow, deliberate motions of the elderly she filled a kettle with water from a jug and set it on the stove to boil.

"So you see, Rebecca isn't here anymore. She came here to see me briefly, urging me to go with her, and then went to England to meet her mother. I don't know where exactly. Lily told me once, but the name escapes me now."

I nodded. "It's okay, I think I know."

"The bundle of letters," Rainey filled in.

"Yes, exactly—Kellerby, England. Dorothea, Rainey found several letters in Becca's dresser drawer at home, all of them from Lily."

Dorothea opened a small canister of Earl Grey tea bags and placed three on a saucer, awaiting the kettle's whistle. "Well, then, my dear, it sounds like you know which way to steer if you want to find Rebecca, but mind you, she may not want to be found just yet."

I started to answer her, but Rainey got there first. "That may be so, but I'm afraid I can't just sit idle knowing my wife's across the Atlantic. Claire, any idea where she might be staying in Kellerby?"

My grandmother replied as I opened my mouth to speak. "When Rebecca left my house a week ago, she made it clear she wanted no one to follow her. Lily is dying, young man, and needs time to complete the ritual. Perhaps you could give them a few more weeks."

The question hung in the air, begging to be asked.

"What ritual?"

Dorothea looked at me, and I saw sorrow, even regret, in her amber eyes. "Something sacred between mother and daughter, I would expect."

Rainey stood to his feet, trying to be polite but clearly impatient. "How do you communicate with the outside world here? I can't get a signal on my cell phone this deep in the woods."

Dorothea turned back to the teakettle, which had begun to squeal, and spoke matter-of-factly. "I've had a phone for quite a few years now if you care to use it.

Ever since the county put in the new road just beyond the trees." She inclined her head in the direction opposite the way Rainey and I had come through the woods. A road we obviously had missed on Aunt Jess's crude map. Seeing Rainey's unsmiling face, Dorothea touched his forearm lightly and made her voice gentle. "But Rebecca most likely wouldn't take your call, you know."

"Yes, I know," Rainey said, his voice gruff as he opened the creaky door to the cottage. He looked back at us. "Claire, do you want to stay and have tea with your grandmother or come with me?" Above the sound of the wind whistling through the trees, I heard the cry of a mockingbird warbling its ironic song. It was one of those moments when time seems to move very slowly. I glanced from Rainey's urgent expression to my grandmother's creased countenance, that odd mixture of intensity and quiet amusement written in her eyes. They both awaited my answer, and I hesitated only a beat—knowing full well I might not see Dorothea again for some time, if at all.

Of course I had to follow Rainey, and of course I knew that his question "Are you coming with me?" meant more than trekking back through the woods. Welcomed or not, I would follow Rainey to Kellerby—the place that had imprinted my girlhood so profoundly, in search of Becca and the piece of my heart planted in the English soil along with Colin's perennials.

The walk back through the woods was silent, much as it had been twenty years ago when Becca, Joe, and I leaned forward into the slapping branches, bound for home, each one lost in his or her own emotions. By some mutual, unspoken consent we said not a word until the woods broke suddenly onto the backyard of my childhood home.

19

En route to England
June 2001

When we were seated on the plane Rainey pulled out the batch of letters from Lily to read again, the ones overnighted by his neighbor Millie and bound with a rubber band.

The flight attendants dimmed the interior plane lights in preparation to show a movie. Ignoring the headsets, I scrunched down in my seat, ordered the letters chronologically, and re-read them by a thin crack of daylight at the bottom of the airplane window.

One letter in the bundle looked to be the most worn, as if Becca had read it over and over until she had memorized its contents.

Rebecca, you don't know how much it meant for me to receive your letter. I may not be able to fly to the States to see you, even though it would be good to see North Carolina again. Some things you can't get out of your blood no matter how hard you try. And believe me, I tried to leave NC, literally and figuratively. I succeeded in the first, but never the second. Now I find I don't even want to leave it—in my mind, that is. Though I'm surrounded by green English hedges and sheep meadows, I still reminisce about my growing-up years in NC. More than anything I long to see you.

If I can't manage the trip, could you make your way to England to meet me?

Your loving mother,

Lily

Kellerby, England

Another letter read:

Rebecca, how will I ever be able to wait until summer to see you? I feel like a little kid counting the days till Christmas. Do you really think you should break away without telling anyone? Disappearing acts always upset those left behind (trust me, I was an expert at this).

Father Maccabee, who has been kind enough to let me stay on his property, is an ancient monk who still writes a sermon by hand every Saturday night, even though he has no flock to preach to and hasn't for 30 years. Dorothea made contact with him a few years ago about the family heirloom and the history behind it. I am glad the pendant found its way to you. Skipping a generation proved to be a wise decision. Anyway, through their many correspondences they struck up a friendship, and when I resurfaced and needed a place to rest—a place to die in peace—your grandmother contacted Father Maccabee and made the arrangements.

So here I am, laid up in England and unable to think of anything but the past—especially the past that might have been with you, my little Rebecca. I sacrificed you on the altar of my freedom, wanting to throw off all those years of captivity in that small quiet house Aunt Jessica found for Dorothea and me. I'm happy at least you never had to grow up making excuses for your mother as I did (how does one explain a recluse to the few school friends she makes?).

No, I have to believe that God worked everything out for the good of us all, even if our *stories are not fully written yet. My own story is drawing to a close, Rebecca, but I think of you, my grown-up daughter, and wonder how many chapters are still waiting to be written in your life. Make them count, my dear one. Make them count.*

The next few letters talked of mundane things, so I skimmed through them quickly. Then my eye settled on the final letter in the batch, dated just one month prior to Becca's disappearance.

Rebecca, Fr Maccabee graciously invited you to come to England and stay with me in one of the vacant rooms here. In a few weeks he wants to perform a sacred ceremony at a church nearby—some observance that apparently will have great meaning for the citizens of this town—and he asked me if I would like to extend the ceremony to include you and me. I said yes . . .

I looked over at Rainey and whispered, "In a town as small as Kellerby, Father Maccabee shouldn't be too hard to find."

"Did you call that church place you were telling me about?"

"The Rectory? Not yet. I barely had time to throw my clothes in the suitcase before we left. I'll call once we land at Heathrow, but it may not be open anymore. It's been twenty years since Becca and I stayed there."

20

Kellerby, England
June 2001

Just the mention of the Rectory flashed that long-ago afternoon across my mind when I came upon Colin Lockwood in the glade behind the inn. Kneeling on the ground planting flowers, he had squinted up at me, his shoulder-length hair pulled back in a ponytail and one earth-brown lock flopping over his right eye. I closed my eyes and settled deeper into my seat. Colin would be long gone by now, the inn sold. I vaguely recalled a letter from Aunt Jess that mentioned Eugenia Lockwood's death a few years ago. With the sale of the inn, Colin would have had the funds to start his own nursery at last.

Arriving in London the next morning I looked for the "water closet" to freshen up while Rainey rented a car. After washing my face and hands I made my way to one of the airport pubs to make the phone call I'd been both anticipating and dreading.

With the adrenaline rush of a schoolgirl, I dialed the odd-looking English phone number to the Rectory and absently pulled the crescent moon pendant from my handbag. The moon's Mona Lisa smile seemed to mock me, and the line rang and rang until I almost hung up.

"Rectory," a female voice said into the phone. "May I help you?"

"Yes," I stammered, "this is Claire Trowling from America. I stayed there a long time ago and wasn't sure the inn was still in operation. But apparently you are."

"Apparently. Looking for a room?"

"Well, actually I need a pair of them for tonight. Staying for several days. Do you have availability?"

I could hear the young woman sigh into the phone. "Hmmm, well, there's the master suite in the front of the house. It's open—and if you stayed here before perhaps you remember it has a small room off to one side with a single bed in it. You could both stay there and still have a bit of privacy."

"Yes, I remember it. That'll work fine." I hesitated a moment. "And be sure to block out several days."

Feeble sunlight broke through the gray cloud cover that morning as I steered our tiny rental car north toward Yorkshire. Once we left the city behind, the rolling countryside broke out beside us in patchwork folds like a quilt thrown over a clothesline. I watched Rainey's reaction to the undulating greenery from the corner of my eye. The English countryside affects almost every American city-dweller the same way, the first time they see it. You forget what land is supposed to look like when you're surrounded by convenience stores and strip shopping centers.

"I still think she should have let me in," Rainey said, and I knew he was talking about Becca. I focused on the road ahead, my mind searching for some kind of consoling answer.

"She's probably doing the best she can, Rain. You'll have a chance to talk things out when you see her." We both watched a flock of birds suddenly lift off a telephone wire and swoop into the sky. Then, following some silent bird cue, the formation changed direction and swooped back the other way, filling the sky momentarily with dark wings. "Becca's had her whole world shift on its axis these past six months."

At the turnoff for Kellerby, the road dipped slightly before we started climbing again. We were in the land of moors, I remembered. After twenty-odd miles I followed the signs and roundabouts to a narrow road bordered on either side by tall hedgerows. We bumped along, making nervous chitchat as we drew closer to our destination. Out of nowhere a gypsy caravan of colorful horse-drawn wagons appeared over a rise, and I was forced to pull onto the shoulder to let them pass.

"Now there's something you don't see every day," Rainey said. "Is there a circus in town?" We nodded and waved to the lead driver of the caravan, who returned our smiles with a stern gaze.

"They were here the time Becca and I visited too.

Must be a good omen," I said, meeting Rainey's eyes for a moment and winking.

He sighed. "At this point I just hope she's safe and that whatever mumbo-jumbo ritual she's about to be involved in won't mess with her head. You know Becca, Claire. She's impressionable."

"Yes, that she is. My sister"—I caught myself, realizing again for the thousandth time that Becca was actually my cousin—"has always had a dramatic flair, but remember that's what you fell in love with, Rain. Back in the early days you couldn't take your eyes off her."

"Still can't."

"I remember watching the two of you together and wishing someone would look at me that way someday—"

"Whoa, watch that pothole," he blurted.

I swerved just in time.

"Somebody will, Claire. He just hasn't found you yet, that's all. Remember that Bible story about the wedding at Cana, when God saved the best for last?" His allusion to Jesus' first miracle, and his more veiled reference to my failed marriage, took me aback for a minute. I realized my eyes were filling with tears again. Good grief, the last thing I wanted was to start slobbering in front of Rainey.

"Hey, now, I didn't mean to make you cry." He stared at me uncomfortably from the passenger seat.

"It's nothing," I lied, blinking, and reached to turn on the radio.

The road inched us toward Kellerby, rolling and curving with the countryside until the small, quaint town rose into view, its few church spires pricking the horizon. From this vantage point Kellerby looked awash in golden light, the beige stones of the older buildings glinting in the pale sunshine. As we descended into the valley that nestled the town on all sides, I glanced around for the road sign marked Gladstone, which would lead us straight to the Rectory. The inn lay on the north side of town, about two miles beyond the town center—an odd occurrence at first glance because churches were always situated in the heart of antiquated towns. But then I remembered the stone church's cursed status and guessed that was why Kellerbians of centuries past gradually moved the town—and its three newer churches—a couple of miles south.

I almost missed it. The clump of wild rosebushes clustered about the inn's forecourt had grown tall in the intervening years, obscuring it. A tangle of other flowering plants dispersed among the roses gave the inn that lovely, haphazard look I had always admired about English gardens. Someone had given the inn a new coat of paint, and it wore an air of vitality missing the last time I saw it.

"You go on inside and register while I get the luggage," Rainey said as I parked the car under a tree.

Instinctively I glanced to the right of the inn; the same pale dirt road ran alongside it and disappeared over a rise, all but veiling the stone church from my view. I could see its spire poking up through the trees.

Pushing open the front door, I mounted the three steps that led up to the main lobby. No one was around, so I rang the bell on the registration desk. After a few minutes the serious young woman I spoke to on the phone rounded the corner and stepped behind the desk. Her stark beauty—long, corn-silk blonde hair pulled back in a ponytail, and two of the bluest eyes I had ever seen—contrasted sharply with her librarian demeanor.

"Ms. Trowling, is it? Pleased to meet you. We have your rooms—well, the master suite—ready if you'd like to go on up. I'll just need you to fill out this form and let me process your credit card."

I produced the necessary information and told her I wanted to stroll around outside for a few minutes. I could hear Rainey talking to someone in the front yard; I ducked down the back hall to the rear of the inn and stepped outside, reentering a place I had visited only in my memory over the past twenty years.

The garden was more beautiful than I remembered it; the new proprietor had obviously spent money making the Rectory grounds lavish. A new fountain stood in the center of the garden, and tasteful gazebos and stone benches were scattered about so that guests could find sanctuary yet still be only seconds from the house. I made my way through an arbor draped in vines, parted the curtain of willow tree branches, and emerged into the tiny glade where I had first talked to Colin. The glade was empty and inviting, but I was in an exploratory mood, so I retraced my steps to the main garden. Locating the gate in the back wall, I headed down the dirt road toward the stone church.

The cluster of trees that shrouded the church upon first approach loomed taller after my absence of two decades. I found a smooth stone in the road and kicked it as I walked along, remembering the first time I walked this dusty path as a girl. Thick with the fringy green growth of summer, the trees blocked my approach as well, so much so that the man weeding around a gravestone set among the older, crumbling headstones jumped as I emerged into view.

I recognized him at once.

Colin Lockwood sprang to his feet and automatically reached down to wipe his palms on the thighs of his faded blue jeans. For one long moment our eyes locked, and I wondered if he remembered me—recognized me—against all odds. The years of working in the sun had streaked his brown hair with lighter strands, and I noted the fine lines around his eyes. His face had grown craggy in the intervening years, but somehow the weathered appearance only made him more attractive.

I was the first to speak.

"I heard your mother died a few years back, Colin. I'm so sorry. I still remember her vividly even after all this time."

He studied me for a moment, his brown eyes glinting in the pale sunlight. And then he nodded and smiled his slow, spreading smile. "Claire Trowling, the little girl with big questions. So you've come back."

My voice came out too husky. "Yes." Silence stretched between us for a few awkward seconds. I rushed to fill the empty space. "You stayed on to run the inn after your mother died? When I called to make the reservations, there was no mention of who the proprietor was. I just assumed—"

"That I'd sell the place? Yes, I almost did. Went away to start my own nursery for a while, but something about the old place kept tugging at me. In the end I decided to kill two birds with one stone. I have a nursery in town. A small establishment, but it makes a tidy profit and allows me to keep my hands in the soil." He inclined his head toward the inn up the dirt road. "So do these grounds. You'll have to see what I've done to our little glade."

"I've just come from there. It's beautiful, Colin." I hesitated for a moment—*He just said "our glade"*—and then found new words. "We just checked in a few minutes ago. My brother-in-law and I came to England to do a bit of . . . research . . . on the Trowling family line. It's more complicated than it sounds, but I knew we needed to start in Kellerby."

He picked up a small sack of garden tools and slung it over his shoulder as he glanced down at his mother's grave. "A lot of things started in Kellerby," he said, his voice gruff, and then signaled me to walk back toward the inn with him.

"Do you miss her very much?"

"Yes, I do. Mum was a character, the way she herded

tourists through the old place like sheep and told her ghost stories over the dinner table." He paused, and I heard a small sigh catch in his throat. "I do miss her. It's funny—growing up you feel at odds with your parents half the time, longing for the day you can move out on your own. Then you really grow up and realize your parents are people too, not just your parents. Of course, for me it was always just her. We actually grew very close during those last few years when her health started to fail."

"I'm sorry." I waited for him to go on. When he didn't I ventured another question. "So now you're running the Rectory alone?"

"That's right."

"The young woman in the office, she's not your . . . ?"

He cocked a sideways smile at me. "No, a hired worker, that's all. Her mother cooks for the inn." His eyes told me he knew what I was thinking.

I focused my gaze up the road and cleared my throat. "I thought you'd be tending the queen's gardens by now. You always had a way with growing things, but I'm glad you came back. The Rectory wouldn't be the same without you." I clamped my mouth shut, alarmed at my bold words.

He laughed. "Yes, gardens will always be one of my finer passions. The ironic thing is that I've felt myself getting pruned and shaped these last several years. And for once the hands doing the pruning weren't mine, if you know what I mean." He glanced back at his mother's headstone, his eyes averted from mine. "It's not easy living alone for so long."

I didn't know what to say to this and so kept quiet.

"Excuse me for prying," he said, looking up, "but will your sister be staying here as well?"

The allure of Becca. I almost gritted my teeth as I lifted my eyes to him.

"You mentioned your brother-in-law, that's all," he said. "I seem to remember your having just the one sister, so naturally I—"

"No, Becca won't be here. She's . . . out of pocket . . . at the moment, but I'm hoping to see her soon." If only he knew the irony of that phrase.

Colin held the back gate to let me pass through first and then led the way through the inn's back door and down the hallway to the lobby. Rainey stood talking to a couple who were just checking in, our luggage still behind him. I grabbed my own suitcase and headed for the stairs.

"Will you two be joining us for lunch today?" Colin called as I mounted the staircase. I mumbled some sort of non-answer and climbed up to the second floor. At that moment all I wanted to do was escape—be alone with my thoughts, which were stirring in a most unsettling way.

The master suite looked virtually unchanged. I threw my suitcase on the giant four-poster bed and stepped into the bathroom to splash cold water on my face, wanting to stop the ridiculous flush that gazed back at me from the mirror. Before a quarter hour passed I crawled into bed and let myself fall into a dead sleep. I dreamed of a young man with an easy, slouching grace sauntering up a dusty dirt road, a purple velvet flute bag slung over his shoulder. Through the cloud of dust kicked up by his feet, I saw him give a casual backward glance—not at me, but at my sister.

21

Kellerby, England
June 2001

The smell of bacon frying woke me, and I immediately thought of Saturday mornings when Mama was still alive. Peering out over the duvet, I saw heavy brocade draperies at a high arched window and unfamiliar wallpaper adorning the walls. As I blinked to clear my eyes, my mind registered where I was. I rolled to a sitting position, looking around for a clock to tell me what time it was. It felt as if I'd been sleeping for days.

After a quick shower, I went downstairs to join the late starters at the breakfast table, grabbed a scone off the side cart instead, and went outside to investigate the grounds. Rainey was nowhere in sight; neither was Colin. Two guests reclined in the garden, reading the *London Times* by the fountain. Nodding hello, I followed the brook toward the back gate and pushed it open, the hinges squeaking as I stepped through. At the bottom of the dirt road that stretched behind the Rectory I found Rainey in the churchyard poking among the headstones. He glanced up, shielding his eyes from the sun with his hand. "Come here, Claire. You should see this one. This headstone dates to the 1500s. Still legible, though barely."

The headstone didn't interest me at the moment. "Have you seen Colin?"

"You mean the owner—the guy with the ponytail?"

"That's the one."

"Yeah, I talked to him first thing this morning. He had to go over to some farm to pick up a load of manure for the garden beds. He should be back soon though. He's easy to talk to. I wound up telling him the real reason why we came to England, you know, the whole story, and he sat there and listened politely without prying. Turns out he can lead us right where we need to go."

"He knows where we can find Becca and Lily?"

"I believe so. It sounds like he's known the old priest they're staying with all his life." Rainey paused for a second and kicked at a clump of sod. "Didn't that old book at the Celtic Muse mention some guy named Lockwood?"

I nodded, my mind turning over his words.

"Well, he must be a great, great relative or other of your friend Colin because our host sure knows a lot about the family history." He shot me a hopeful look. "Claire, she's here—close by—I can feel it."

"I know what you mean. I feel it too. When Colin gets back I'll ask him to take us to the priest's house."

"Well that's just it," he said. "I already did, and he said he wanted to talk to you first." He met my eyes, that same pleading look visible in their depths. "I'm not sure what that's all about."

"Neither am I, but I'll find out and let you know, okay? Meanwhile, since you're down here I want to show you something." I walked toward the far side of the church and gestured for Rainey to follow. I didn't have to search long to find it—the devil face carved into a large stone of the church's western wall.

"Is that what I think it is?" Rainey said, stooping to peer at the strange visage. "A gargoyle in relief?"

"You could call it that." I reached out to touch the carved face. "Colin told me the story behind this place the summer I turned fourteen." Rainey listened eagerly as I told him the tale of a grief-ravaged priest who hanged himself in the bell tower, the horrified villagers who found him three days later on Sunday morning, the Druidic cult that met on the church grounds by the light of full moons, and the priest half a century later who reclaimed the stone church for God.

Rainey squinted up at the gray stone bell tower as I finished. "Whoa, I thought I heard some good stories back around the Boy Scout campfires, but this one beats all."

"It certainly does," Colin said, striding toward us from around the southern wall of the church, a grin stretched across his face. We both turned to look at him. My pulse quickened as it always did when he was near. He met my eyes and held them for a second before addressing Rainey.

"I just got back and came to find you, Mr. Garrett. Did a bit of thinking while I was gone and believe I've remembered something you'll want to hear. But now that I see Claire is here, do you mind if I have a word with her first?" His brown eyes gazed at me expectantly. I looked at Rainey; he saw the question in my eyes and nodded.

"Go ahead. I can wait a little while longer—whatever it takes to make this thing happen."

We left Rainey poking among the headstones once again as Colin led me across a field that adjoined the Rectory's property and beyond to a knoll that overlooked a view. We sat cross-legged on the grass side by side.

"Takes your breath away, doesn't it?" he said after a few moments of silence. All I could do was stare at the spectacle of nature before me. Surrounding us on three sides were sloping meadows awash in brilliant yellow—rapeseed blossoms in full bloom. Here and there a patch of bright green grass peeked through, and the pale blue horizon settled over the landscape soft as a baby's blanket.

I looked at his profile. "So what is it you needed to talk to me about, Colin?"

He kept his gaze on the horizon as he spoke. "Your brother-in-law filled me in on the real purpose for your trip to England. He also showed me the letter sent to his wife by her mother, this person named Lily who apparently lives right here in Kellerby." Colin turned to look me in the eye. "Do you know the story behind this jewelry, Claire?"

"A little. I read about it in an old book at a Celtic shop back home. It told all about Pritchard and Thornsby and said an earl from Queen Elizabeth's court commissioned a handful of crescent moon pieces with inset rubies. The book even mentioned someone with your last name—a Chastain Lockwood."

Colin's eyes dilated. "You know more than I realized. But do you know what happened to the jewelry in the late 1500s? To the pendant especially?"

I shook my head.

He leaned back on his elbows and pinned me with his gentle gaze. "You obviously remember the story of the bell tower and what happened in 1560—I just heard you tell it quite captivatingly to your brother-in-law."

"Yes," I said, waiting for him to go on.

"Well, there's more to the story. The same year the rector of St. Barnabas hanged himself, all havoc broke loose in Kellerby. The townspeople shunned the church property, calling it cursed. Some refused to walk past it down the road, or even tend to the graves of their ancestors in the churchyard. On the first full moon after the horrible event a local farmer with neighboring property was awakened in the night by a strange noise. He went to investigate and followed the sound all the way to the churchyard, where he saw a group of Druids chanting in a circle. Legend has it he ran home to tell his wife, but he never made it. He fell in a ditch and drowned in two feet of water. A young member of the Druids followed him at a distance, you see, and thus the story survived. That young man was the one you just mentioned, my ancestor Chastain Lockwood.

"The Druidic group required total secrecy whenever and wherever they gathered. The reputation for the land being cursed gave the cult the cloak of secrecy it needed, and so they continued to meet there for a long time—a half century in fact.

"As you may recall, Lockwood was apprenticed to Thornsby after Pritchard's death, and so he had access to the goldsmithy's records and knowledge of its commissions by the Court. Some hold that a royal henchman assassinated Pritchard when he refused to do another commission—why, we may never know. Lockwood would have known the value of the pendants, and apparently the last one had not yet been delivered to the earl at the time of Pritchard's death. In the troubling weeks and months after his partner's death, Thornsby forgot about the pendant it would seem, but Lockwood did not. He pilfered it for his own use.

"You must remember that the Druids were Celtic, a religious sect if you will, though more pagan than anything else. Lockwood was an avowed member of the local clan, and so when the grand master announced a ritual to seal the site of St. Barnabas—especially the graveyard grounds—for their own use, Lockwood supplied the most valuable Celtic symbol he possessed, the crescent moon pendant with the royal ruby."

Colin stood to his feet suddenly and reached out his hand to pull me up. "Let's walk for a bit, shall we? There's a beautiful meadow I want to show you."

As he led me down the steep grassy slope he kept hold of my hand. I hoped he would forget to drop it when we reached level ground again. At the bottom of the hill we meandered through low-hanging dogwood branches heavy with white blossoms, forded a stream by stepping stones, and found a low flat rock in the sun. The meadow Colin had promised spread open before us, a riot of purple, yellow, pink, red, and blue wildflowers swaying in the light breeze.

We settled on the rock, and he picked up his narrative. "And now let me come to the end of the story, the part that might involve you and your sister. When your brother-in-law told me she and her mother were to take part in a ritual at a holy site, I realized it could only mean one thing. You see, as the decades went by, the Druidic clan that met on the church grounds grew thinner in numbers, perhaps by simple attrition. When a new priest moved to Kellerby in the early 1600s, fifty years after the priest of St. Barnabas hanged himself in the bell tower, he naturally heard the story and the reason why people shunned the church. Filled with righteous indignation that pagans should be allowed to take over land consecrated to God, this bold man waged a campaign to expel the Druids and was in fact successful. He reconsecrated the church to God and held nightly vigils for so long that the Druidic clan was frustrated in its attempts to gather there. Every time they crept toward St. Barnabas under cover of night, they met with the bright light of the elderly priest, holding aloft a lantern in the bell tower and quoting Scripture loudly. He claimed he was shining forth the light of Christ, who charged his followers to be like a city on a hill or a burning light, not hidden under a bushel but shining for all the world to see.

"Lockwood had grown into an old man by now, and as people did in those days, he still lived in the town where he was born. One of the last remaining Druids in Kellerby, he served as grand master in his final years and certainly incurred the wrath of the new priest—until something remarkable happened. Within a year Chastain Lockwood had a late-life Damascus Road experience. He writes about it in his journals."

Colin reached back to undo his ponytail and ran his hand through his hair. Just barely shoulder length, it glinted in the sunlight, and I tried not to stare.

"The entire story is recorded in Lockwood's own handwriting. He set out to read the Gospels to disprove Christianity from a purely intellectual ground. In the process he became the most fervent believer. He didn't live long after his conversion to Christianity. As he lay dying he asked his grown son, Clive, to fetch something from his bureau. He brought the pendant to him and listened as Lockwood told him the story behind the jewelry—how it was commissioned by a royal but also the part it played in an unholy ceremony. Lockwood placed it in his son's hands and told him he wanted him to have it, but only if he had the object blessed by a priest. And that, of course, is where Lockwood's own journal record ceases. Clive started the tradition of passing it down the generations as a family heirloom. Years later a descendant was going through Clive Lockwood's letters posthumously and found a fragment of writing that recorded his father's last words to him: 'Bless the church, my dear son. Promise me you will bless the church.' No one today seems to know if he ever carried out his father's dying wish."

Colin looked at me and waited for my reaction. When I said nothing, he went on. "But Father Bernard plans to do so, one week from now. So you see, you and Rainey arrived just in time for what promises to be an historic event in our little town—the ritual of reconsecration of St. Barnabas."

As Colin came to the end of his story my mind rushed to fill in the blanks. Of course. The holy ritual of consecration would hold significance for Becca and her newfound mother too—a baptism and a requiem all in one.

22

Kellerby, England
June 2001

By mutual agreement we started the walk back to the Rectory, Colin again taking my hand as we climbed the steep grassy hillside.

"There's only one other person in Kellerby who knows the story as thoroughly as I do, and it was his library I visited this morning to do a little fact checking. My historian friend is the priest who's giving sanctuary to your sister and her mother. His name is Father Bernard Maccabee, and he's been tracking the whereabouts of the crescent moon pendant for years. An old woman from America named Dorothea contacted Father Maccabee and told him the pendant had resurfaced. Apparently he later made contact with Rebecca's mother Lily and that's how she came to be here."

Back at the Rectory's grounds, Colin went to find Rainey—we had been gone so long I doubted he was still in the churchyard—and I hurried inside the inn, my heart stirred from all he had told me. From what Colin had said, Becca was very close by indeed, and Rainey and I would likely see her in the next few days unless she insisted on prolonging her seclusion. How would it be between us, I wondered. Would she smile and run to me for a sisterly hug the way she always did when we were apart and then reunited? Or would she hold back, her gold-flecked eyes smoldering because we ignored her wishes and pursued her across the Atlantic? As far as Becca knew, I was still clueless about our being cousins. Would the knowledge she possessed, and my presumed ignorance of it, change her behavior toward me, or would our long history as sisters prevail in the end? Where did the ground between blood sisters end and the wide plain of lifelong friends begin? If this season of our lives were to transcend the startling element that always accompanies discovery, and move into an easy new grace, it would require maturity and love in equal parts from both of us.

And Lily—what would it be like to put a face to the name in Aunt Jess's fantastic story? The runaway favored daughter, favored over my own mother, but made good in the end. From what I read in her letters to Becca, life had wrought a woman of substance, perhaps despite her efforts to the contrary. Living could do that to you.

I pulled on a hoodie, changed into my running shoes, and went down the steep staircase to the ground floor. I left a note at the front desk informing Rainey that I was taking a jog into town. The two-mile run would do me good and help clear my head. Outside the air was still crisp; I had forgotten how chilly English summers can be. A quarter mile into the run my long limbs started to warm and my body clicked into that comfortable autopilot gear that I knew would carry me into Kellerby and back again.

The country highway that led to town rose and dipped and then nearly plunged as it curled into the quaint town center with its golden-brown stonework. Seen from up here, Kellerby always struck me as a miniature landscape from a needlepoint wall hanging. Instinctively I leaned backward and used my calves and heels as brake pads to slow my descent.

A small black car slowed suddenly on its approach from town. I looked up and found myself staring straight into the eyes of Phineas Culver, the odd little man who offered to buy the crescent moon pendant at the Celtic Muse shop. I knew he recognized me. Slowing to a walk, I moved onto the cobblestone sidewalk and ventured a backward glance. The black car was making a U-turn, obviously about to head back in my direction. What did Phineas Culver want with me, other than the pendant? And out of all the towns in England, what was the likelihood he would live in the very one I was visiting?

I didn't feel like talking to him, or being pressured about the jewelry, so I ducked into the nearest store I saw—a fabric and dress shop—and tried to hide myself among the tall bolts of material. A woman with lacquered blonde hair approached, smiling. "May I help you? My dear, are you all right? You look like you've seen a ghost."

Still winded from my run, I took a deep breath and asked her if she had a phone I could borrow.

Her smile drew into a thin line. "Local call?"

"Yes. The Rectory, in fact. That's where I'm staying."

"Oh, Eugenia's old place—poor dear. She suffered terribly in her last years. But I hear that handsome son of hers is doing a fine job of running the inn. Are you staying for long?"

"I—I'm not really sure yet," I stammered. "Probably not, if everything works out. Where did you say your phone is?"

She took the hint and led me to a back room strewn with bolts of fabric and dressmaker's busts. I dialed the Rectory and waited while the girl at the front desk went to find Rainey. He had just come inside a few minutes ago and couldn't be far, she said. While I held the line, I heard the bell on the door of the fabric shop jingle as someone came inside. I hoped it wasn't Phineas Culver.

Rainey sighed into the phone as I told him my predicament. "Claire, where are you? I'll come and pick you up. Colin wants to show us both something anyway—some library he mentioned earlier. I think it's on the same property where Becca's staying. Now, tell me again, where exactly are you?"

I gave Rainey directions to the dress shop and hung up the phone. The store seemed quiet so I ventured out from my hiding place. The woman with lacquered blonde hair glanced up from a rack of clothes she was straightening.

I smiled at her. "Thank you for letting me use your phone, ma'am. Do you mind if I wait here for a friend? He's coming to pick me up—I'm not quite up to the jog back to the Rectory."

She shook her head. "I should say not. Why on earth would you want to pound the pavement when there are perfectly good vehicles available? I can't believe you young people today. Women never ran when I was a girl. But to each his own. Of course you can stay. Always nice to have a customer. May I interest you in anything while you wait?"

"I'll have a look," I said politely and headed toward a rack at the back of the store to browse a new crop of summer blouses.

Ten minutes passed before Rainey showed up, gesturing to me from the doorway. Outside I saw not the rental car we'd driven from Heathrow but Colin's red pickup truck idling at the curb.

Rainey held the door open, and I slid into the middle of the seat, glad for a chance to sit close to Colin. He smelled earthy and good. I swallowed hard as he pulled away from the curb and steered the truck past Kellerby's five blocks of downtown. He took the road that wound upward on the far side of town, glancing over to smile at me.

"Rainey says you want to show us a library. Would

this happen to be the private library you told me about this morning?"

Colin nodded and answered his cell phone, which rang as he was about to speak to me. "Sure thing. We'll be right there. Tell Father Bernard to be ready for us."

Colin accelerated up the steep road and then fell into a casual conversation with Rainey about growing crops in the Yorkshire soil. I watched the rolling landscape move past our windows as he pointed out the different crops growing in the rich farmland. The road leveled out on higher ground, and we took a sudden swerve left onto a smaller bumpy road that wound for a mile or two before ending abruptly at the gates of an ancient stone edifice, its chapel spire piercing the treetops. I could see several other buildings beyond the chapel, all constructed of the same bronze-colored stone. A very old-looking sign read St. Sebastian's Monastery.

I waited to scoot across the seat so I could explore the monastery. Colin stepped out of the pickup and handed me down as if I were a lady in a carriage. His eyes danced with mischief, and I could see how much he was enjoying my anticipation.

Rainey gave a low whistle and moved out ahead of us, calling back over his shoulder, "You Brits sure know how to play the antiquity card, don't you? Claire, can you believe this place? It's like something out of a . . . a . . ."

I helped him out. "An Anthony Trollope novel?"

"Exactly, except I never heard of the guy."

Colin and I laughed, and he quickened his pace to catch up with Rainey like a tour guide. "Before I show you the library, you'll have to promise to follow a few ground rules. This place is off-limits to tourists, and so they're not used to having many visitors. The monks—or at least the few who are left—make an exception for old friends, however. The first and most important rule is to keep the volume of your voice low."

"What's the second rule?" Rainey wanted to know.

"No gum chewing on the premises."

He led us past the chapel, which brooded over the grounds as cool and dark as a tomb. Beyond the chapel a series of lower-roofed buildings fanned out, and Colin steered us toward the grandest structure of them all. We stepped through its ornate arched stone doorway, and I knew at once we had entered the monastery's scriptorium.

The dim interior smelled of old books, and a cloying mustiness clung to everything. Though our eyes had barely adjusted to the dark interior, Colin plunged ahead, leading us through a cavernous room filled floor to ceiling with books and scrolls, some of them several hundred years old, I guessed. Luckily I was wearing my jogging shoes, but the sound of the guys' hard-soled footsteps echoed off the walls. On the other side of the room we came to a hallway with a spiral staircase that led straight up. I peered upward but couldn't see the top.

"This way," Colin said, leaping onto the third step of the staircase and climbing fast. Rainey and I followed single file. Colin was already two full spirals ahead of us, and his voice echoed softly as he called down to us. "Father Bernard is looking forward to meeting you two. I told him as much of your story as I could remember. Sorry. I hope that was permissible."

"Sounds like he already knows most of the story from what I hear," Rainey said.

"Yes, more than you might realize. He's an historian as well as the retired abbot of St. Sebastian's Monastery. He's lived within these walls since he was twenty-two years old, and now he's as old as Methuselah."

I was about to respond when the spiral staircase opened suddenly onto a landing that fed into a long hallway. From the hallway several doors led into rooms holding who knew what, but Colin didn't allow us to wonder for long. He was already making his way to the far end of the hallway, speaking low as he padded toward the heavy walnut door.

Inside, a world created for book lovers met my eyes—a long rectangular room with windows running the length of one side, each with a wooden window seat overlooking an exquisite view. The ground dropped away suddenly on this side of the monastery, and looking out one saw a host of towering trees clustered close to the scriptorium, each thickly garbed in summertime green lacework.

I turned to gaze at all four sides of the room—several high wooden desks with sloping tops were situated around the perimeter, and everywhere I looked stood stacks of books and scrolls. Earthenware pottery jars at each desk contained long thin paintbrushes that probably hadn't been used in decades. Paints, bits of torn parchment, and blotters confirmed to me where we were. I turned to Colin, aware that my eyes must be shining.

"Colin, this is where the monks illuminated the Scriptures, isn't it?" My voice came out a whisper.

He smiled and nodded. "Yes, love, I was hoping you would figure it out without my telling you. This is a room not very many people from the outside get to see. Truly a magnificent room when you consider its history. Tuck it away in your memory because you may never see it again. Right through here, please."

He led us past the high sloping desks to a small door in the corner I hadn't noticed before. Colin tapped on the door, and an elderly male voice answered, "Please come in, it's open."

As the door creaked open Colin stepped back to allow me to enter first, and I found myself staring into the pale eyes of a man who looked a century old. Though cloudy, his eyes held an unmistakable spark in them, and he smiled broadly. He clasped my outstretched hand in both of his. "Welcome, my dear, welcome. I've been looking forward to your visit all morning, ever since my young friend here called." He inclined his bald head toward Colin. "I'm Father Bernard Maccabee, the former abbot of this crumbling old ruin—and your most devoted servant."

Father Bernard's smile was infectious, and I returned it warmly, making introductions for Rainey and me.

Though he walked with a slight stoop, the priest appeared wiry and energetic for a centenarian. His long black cassock swooshed as he led us toward a table set for tea against a bow window.

"Please, do sit down. Even a monk must take his tea now and then, providing he's English. I've had the cook prepare some lovely little teacakes in honor of your visit—quite a rarity for St. Sebastian's, I assure you. How do you take your tea?"

As Father Bernard prattled on, I started to wonder if this visit was really about historical documents rather than a social call for a lonely, aged man. We drank tea and made small talk for nearly forty-five minutes before the priest rang a bell and had the tea service cleared away. As soon as the attending monk left the room, Father Bernard turned toward us, suddenly serious.

"Colin told me why you've come here to England." He looked at Rainey, his eyes full of compassion. "I know you're anxious to see your wife, Mr. Garrett. She is safe and not far from where we're sitting, but her mother Lily—a delightful woman—is dying as we speak. When Rebecca came here to England over a week ago, she knew it was a farewell journey. A journey of acquaintance and awakening, and one full of meaning for her, but also a journey of farewell—a journey toward the grave, literally, for the mother she just met. She asked that I keep her whereabouts secret until such time she chose to reveal them. Rebecca knows that you and Claire are here—and she also knows you will undoubtedly take part in a sacred ceremony next Sunday. Give her these last few days alone with Lily before you take her back home, I beg of you. Once Rebecca crosses back over the Atlantic, she knows she will never see her mother again—this side of heaven."

The room plunged into silence. I could hear a distant clock ticking somewhere, and the sound swelled and magnified in the lengthening quiet. We all exchanged glances, each not sure who should speak first. It was Colin who finally did. He looked directly at me as he spoke.

"I only learned of your sister's story this morning when I spoke to Mr. Garrett"—he nodded toward Rainey—"and Father Bernard. I know you two have come a long way to find Rebecca, and perhaps to put things to rights between you. Trust me when I say that everything will come out right in the end, and very soon as Father Bernard indicated."

"Yes," the old monk said. "So are we agreed we can wait till Sunday next? If so, I will digress for a moment to other matters."

Rainey looked at me and reached across to clasp my hand before nodding to Father Bernard.

"Colin also mentioned that you have the crescent moon pendant in your possession, but I'm sure that's not what you've come to see me about." His ancient eyes twinkled as he reached for a phone and spoke into the mouthpiece. "Please bring the documents in now, Phinn. Yes, we're ready."

He met our eyes once more. "You see, from my young monk days I've been fascinated with history, and so care of the library fell to my keeping. The Lockwood family history and how it pertains to Pritchard and Thornsby's last commission—the crescent moon pendant—is well known to many Kellerby citizens, especially the older ones." He pinned me with his gaze before going on. "This jewelry is valuable, but that fact alone is not the reason for my little speech right now."

He paused for effect, looking at each one of us in turn, then settling on Rainey. "I would like to ask your permission to bless the pendant and use it in the ceremony of reconsecration at St. Barnabas next week. At the same time, your wife Rebecca asked me to conduct a ritual of blessing for her and Lily." He looked at me and beamed. "She would like you to participate too, Ms. Trowling."

Rainey and I exchanged glances, and I knew instantly what he was thinking—more hocus-pocus—but I dispelled it with a smile. I was about to say something in reply when the door opened and a small thin man with wire-rimmed glasses came in carrying a leather portfolio bulging with documents. It was Phineas Culver.

"Mr. Culver!" It was too late to try to keep alarm out of my voice. "Are you stalking me?"

Father Bernard laughed heartily, cutting off Culver's reply. "That he is, my dear, that he is. But have no fear. My good assistant would never want to alarm you. After the jeweler in North Carolina contacted us about the crescent moon heirloom, I sent Phineas to inspect it personally.

"When Phineas realized you had the pendant he naturally tried to acquire it monetarily. But you refused to sell it, Mr. Garrett, and for understandable reason—it has extreme sentimental value to you." The old monk nodded to Phineas Culver. Taking his cue, the small man adjusted the glasses on his nose and opened the bulky portfolio, pulling out various genealogical documents and old photographs as he spoke.

"The heirloom in your sister's possession has a long history in the Lockwood family and its various branches down through the centuries—including your branch, Ms. Trowling. As you can imagine, the tradition of passing the jewelry to a daughter in the family made it doubly difficult to track, what with all the name changes. That's how we lost track of its whereabouts once the jewelry crossed the Atlantic. For a time it appeared to have been lost to antiquity for good, but when we received information about the pendant from the Celtic Muse, everything quickly fell into place. I believe Colin told you the crescent moon pendant's dark history and how Chastain Lockwood implored his son to 'bless the church.' He had become a Christian himself by this time, and we believe it was his intention to bless the object itself, along with the church, as an act of faith and blessing over the family line."

Father Bernard nodded, his eyes full of light. "Yes, yes, and so you see, my dears, that's why we want to use the pendant in the reconsecration ceremony. I asked Rebecca if she would allow me to place it on the altar, but in her haste to come to England she forgot to bring it. I trust you have it with you, Ms. Trowling. If so, I believe Rebecca wants to wear it around her neck that day. Symbolically, perhaps."

Phineas Culver cleared his throat. "It's not every day that a lost jewel of this magnitude is recovered from antiquity. But for me there are more personal matters pressing at the moment. You see, I'm a direct descendant of the priest who first reconsecrated St. Barnabas—the stone church behind the Rectory. His name was Matthew Phineas Culver. I am his namesake in more ways than one, and as I saw the church fall into disuse in my boyhood, I vowed to carry out the ritual of reconsecration someday."

Once more silence filled the room. Father Bernard leaned back in his chair and clasped his hands across his frail midsection. The large cross he wore around his neck caught a shaft of sunlight streaming through the window and glinted with the up-and-down rhythm of his breathing. Rainey leaned forward, his elbows propped on the table. "So what exactly will this ceremony involve? And what's our part in it?"

Father Bernard's crinkled old face stretched into a slow smile. "Ah, I thought you would never ask."

23

Kellerby, England
June 2001

On a Sunday morning in June the citizens of Kellerby awoke to the sound of a soft rain pattering on their rooftops. Lifting the edges of their curtains and blinds, they saw a solid gray sky that promised no letup of the drizzle. From the master suite window at the Rectory I saw the same thing, but instead of plunging into a somber mood I felt almost childishly buoyant. So many things would culminate on this day, and others were just beginning. I thought of how much had changed in my own life in one short week: losing a sister and gaining a sister-cousin; discovering a grandmother I never knew I had; finding out about an aunt (Lily) I didn't know existed; seeing more deeply into the nature of the mother I'd lost over a decade ago. And Colin—well, for whatever duration, for whatever God intended, he was back in my life after an absence of twenty years. If all went as planned, the town of Kellerby would also regain the life of its oldest church on this remarkable day.

The Internet has nothing on old-fashioned word of mouth when a noteworthy event is about to happen, and the reconsecration of St. Barnabas surely fit that bill.

In the intervening days since our visit to St. Sebastian's Monastery, the town of Kellerby crackled to life in preparation for the ceremony. Shopkeepers posted hand-lettered signs in their shop windows urging locals and tourists alike to rally around the stone church Sunday morning. The more mercenary merchants milked the church's dark history by peddling all manner of Druidic objects and scheduled ghost tours of the town. Kellerby's other churches held bazaars to raise last-minute funds needed to feed the crowd after the ceremony. The local women's club produced a wedding tent, folding chairs and tables, balloons, and giant streamers for the lawn after-party.

I realized just how much the spirit of revelry and anticipation filled the town of Kellerby when I drove in on Thursday to pick up some spices and fresh produce from an open-air market. Colin was off tending to his nursery business, Rainey was doing work on his laptop for his job back home, and the daylight hours stretched long and lazy ahead of me. Desperate for an errand, I had asked Tilda, the Rectory's cook, to give me something to do.

"Everyone else is busy with preparations," I sighed, propping my elbows on her canning table. "I'll go mad if I have to sit here one more minute doing nothing."

Tilda pushed a wisp of gray hair out of her glistening face with her forearm, her hands covered in flour. Beside her sat a bowl of sugared elderberries she would bake into the piecrust she had rolled out on the table's smooth wooden surface. "Ha! I'd give my eyeteeth for nothing to do right now. You want something to do? I'll certainly accommodate you. Can you take dictation?"

I looked at her, startled, for a moment until she broke into a toothy grin. "Oh, go on with you, not that kind of dictation, silly. I need fresh fruits and vegetables for all those delicacies I'll be whipping up tomorrow. Got two of my nieces coming in to help me prepare the food, but those veggies won't get bought by themselves. How about you go into town and fetch them for me?"

I wrote swiftly as Tilda rattled off the produce and spices she needed. Such a long marketing list would keep me busy for quite a while—all the better, I reasoned.

I pulled the rental car to the curb in downtown Kellerby and hopped out, tucking a large marketing basket on my arm. I looked up and down the main street that ran through town. The usually languid town was teeming with people despite the work hour. The market Tilda preferred sat on the north end of the street, so I headed in that direction.

As I approached Swanson's Bakery a counter clerk huffed out the front door with a small table and stocked it with petit fours, cakes, and other pastries. A sandwich board propped on the sidewalk read "Donations for St. Barnabas." The clerk looked up as I passed by, peered at me closely for a second, and then grew wide-eyed. "You're that American staying at Eugenia's place, aren't you? I heard you're in town for the big ceremony Sunday noon."

"I'm sorry, have we met?" I stammered.

"Janey—Janey Smithton." The woman extended her hand and pumped my own vigorously. "So you traveled all the way from Florida to attend the reconsecration ceremony? Oh, it promises to be quite a shindig, ma'am, I'm sure. How did you come to hear about it? Did you know Eugenia? Of course, now the Rectory is run by her son—a quiet but capable one, he is. Father Bernard told Father Desmond—he's the vicar of St. Eustace, my own church, just two blocks away—that he'd be mighty blessed if we all got behind the celebration, so I'm trying to do my part."

She took a breath and indicated the pastry-laden table. I seized my chance. "So you're raising funds to help with . . . ?"

"The cost of the celebration, and Father Bernard has asked anyone interested to start a restoration fund for the old church as well." Her heavy-lidded eyes turned wistful. "My own mum attended St. Barnabas when we was just little things. I have vague memories of my brothers and me swinging our legs from them old pews and running through the graveyard while Mum chatted after service. She always got so steamed at us for doing that—said it was disrespectful of the dead, but what's the dead mean to a bunch of energetic young things such as we were?"

She sighed and seemed to remember me standing there. "Will I see you at the ceremony then, on Sunday? I hear—" she paused, groping for words—"I hear there's a deeper meaning to the ceremony for you, ma'am, if you'll pardon my saying so."

I blinked. "What do you mean?" Surely she didn't know the story of Becca and me—and of Lily too.

"Your sister and all," Janey said in a hushed tone. "I'll be praying that everything comes out right in the end."

Strange—Janey Smithton had just uttered the very same words Colin said at the monastery about this extraordinary journey to find Becca. It was still my hope, my prayer, that everything would "come out right in the end."

I smiled and thanked her, then moved on down the sidewalk toward the vegetable market. Another shopkeeper saw me approaching from a distance and hailed me like a cab. "We'll see you on Sunday!" he called. "The ceremony at St. B's has everyone in a happy dither."

Could it be the entire town was taking part—and knew the details of my own role in this developing drama? "Yes, it's wonderful, isn't it?" I called back, smiling. "I'll be there." As I moved along the sidewalk other people caught my eye and smiled or nodded shyly in my direction. The Kellerby merchants had used every imaginable approach to fund-raising for St. Barnabas, from sidewalk flower sales to antiques raffles to a dunking booth featuring the mayor. I glimpsed the poor man clambering onto the collapsible seat, soaking wet after yet another good aim.

When I turned the corner at Lombard Street I nearly crashed headlong into an Anglican minister, his white clerical collar and black suit starched to a crisp finish. "Ho, there! Forgive me, my dear, I didn't mean to—are you the young lady who's staying at the Rectory? The American? I don't mean to pry, but the whole town is talking about the upcoming ceremony, you see, and someone pointed you out to me when you came to town a few days ago."

"Yes, I'm Claire Trowling," I said, warming to the minister's good-natured manner. "I can't believe everyone seems to know me here."

"Oh, you've become quite the local celebrity, I'm afraid, and on short notice too. Forgive my rudeness. I'm Father Desmond, vicar of St. Eustace over there." He shook my hand and nodded toward a church constructed of the same beige stone much of Kellerby was built from. It was ornate and old, but I judged it to be younger than St. Barnabas with its time-worn stones and bizarre devil face.

The vicar eyed my basket. "Looks like you've come to do some marketing. Tilda sent you on an errand, did she? I can direct you to the best vegetable vendors. Of course, don't tell anyone I said so, but there are one or two you'll want to steer clear of—bruised produce and all."

Father Desmond turned and walked with me toward the fruit and vegetable market, apparently forestalling whatever errand had first brought him into Lombard

Street. As we ambled along he discreetly indicated the best produce vendors and selected the ripest fruit and vegetables for me. He made arrangements to have the many pounds of heavier produce delivered to the Rectory, tossing only the lighter items in my basket.

His forehead suddenly creased in concentration. "I suppose you've heard the story of St. Barnabas's dark history."

I nodded. "Yes, Colin told me."

A fruit vendor looked up from her wares as we passed by. "Afternoon, vicar."

"Why, hello, Millicent. Business doing well?"

"Never sold so many melons on a Thursday in my life, as I can remember," the woman said, smiling broadly.

"Excellent, excellent. We'll be seeing you on Sunday then."

He picked up the thread of our conversation as we left Millicent's fruit stand behind. "Well, then, if Colin filled you in, I won't bore you with my version of St. B's ancient history. The church's more recent past is what concerns me most, and it's why I was so delighted to hear of the reconsecration ceremony. Father Bernard is a spiritual father to me, and Phineas Culver is my nephew. Hmm, I can see by your expression you've met the young man. Well, don't be put off by Phinny. He's a good-hearted chap, if somewhat diffident."

I ignored the comment about Phineas Culver. "But you lead another parish here in town. Weren't you worried . . . ?"

"You mean the old sheep-stealing concern? No, I've no worries in that regard. Nothing would make me happier than to see St. B's resurrected as a house of worship. My fellow clergymen and I are just sheepdogs, as Father Bernard reminds us, not the real shepherd. And believe me, there are enough citizens to fill all three churches in Kellerby, plus St. B's, if people were so inclined."

Father Desmond took my elbow in the old-fashioned manner and steered me back toward the main street through Kellerby. "I attended St. B's when I was a boy—that was before the last vicar fled in grief after his wife died. By degrees the church fell into disuse and disrepair, I'm afraid. The old stories started circulating again, and it was easier for folks to just avoid it in favor of the churches here in the town center."

He was silent for a moment. "Did you know this Sunday will be the first time the bell in that ancient bell tower has been rung in, what, thirty, forty years? I don't care if half the fanfare is generated by the Historical Society. God will have the last say in the history of St. B's, you can rest assured."

We reached my car, and I thanked Father Desmond for his help in the produce marketing. "Please be sure to say hello this Sunday after the ceremony. I'll introduce you to my brother-in-law and hopefully my—"

I broke off, catching myself, but he finished for me. "Your sister, perhaps? And someone new to you besides?" The vicar's eyes crinkled in a smile. "Don't you worry about a thing, my dear. They're both in good hands.

Father Bernard assures me of that. The family crisis that brought you here to England has spawned good things. I have a feeling quite a few stories will come full circle this Sunday."

He stood on the sidewalk in his crisp black suit and waved me good-bye as I U-turned into traffic and headed back to the Rectory, my heart filled with a new anticipation. After the conversation with Father Desmond I felt stirred, realizing the profound truth of his words. I also felt a profound need to return to the monastery, if not to see and speak with Becca (for I had promised to wait), then at least to be where she was and soak up the sacred atmosphere of the place.

After dropping the basketful of produce at the Rectory I drove out to St. Sebastian's Monastery, past the rolling farmland and along the curving, bumpy road that led to the monastery campus. I parked under the low-hanging boughs of a shade tree and decided to explore the grounds on foot. If my presence seemed to go unnoticed—or at least unminded by the few monks who resided there—I might venture back into the scriptorium and the massive library.

The monastery campus was alive with blooming things, and everywhere I looked the landscape was suffused with the rich green of English grass. I followed a footpath around the corner of the dining hall to a side courtyard with a trickling fountain and potted trees. An archway in the far wall of the courtyard led to the steeply sloping ground Rainey and I had spied from the second-story illumination chamber. The ground was treacherously steep—more so even than it appeared from the higher view—so I backtracked through the courtyard and explored the other side of the monastery instead.

The grounds on the west side included an herb garden, a vegetable garden, a small amphitheater with a cross in the foreground and stone slabs for seats, a compost area, and a small enclosed graveyard nearly obscured behind a clump of trees. As I headed there to read the gravestone markers, the sound of a soft sob reached my ears.

I turned to follow the sound, just beyond the border of trees, and emerged into yet another garden—this one a profusion of flowers, with a small reflecting pond. Someone was reflecting there, all right, a thin, frail-looking woman in a wheelchair, her back to me.

I didn't need to see her face to know who it was. Lily heard a twig snap under my feet and turned with a slight gasp, her beautiful face registering alarm followed by recognition and then delight.

She brushed the tears away quickly. "Claire? Oh my goodness, is that you?"

"Yes, it's me." I smiled shyly, not knowing what else to say to this stranger who was so closely tied to me through Becca.

She wheeled her chair to face me and held out her arms. "Please, give me a hug. I would stand if I had the strength, but today's been one of my bad days."

I stooped and hugged her, resting my chin on her bony

shoulder. "I see Becca in you," I said, my voice barely a whisper.

"Hey, now, none of that." She pulled back and gave me a mock-stern look of reproach. "Even if I am an invalid, there's no need to whisper around me. I've so been looking forward to meeting you, Claire. You have no idea. Becca's told me all the stories I could pull out of her, about your childhood, your teenage years, your marriage—sorry, I didn't mean to say that."

"It's all right. I hardly think of it anymore. But, Lily, I want to hear about you. Here I was not expecting to meet you until this Sunday at the reconsecration ceremony."

I sat on the cool grass beside her, and we both turned toward the reflecting pond. "I suppose I'm trespassing in a way," I began. "I promised Father Bernard I would give you and Becca time alone before intruding."

"A wonderful intrusion, if you ask me." Her amber eyes danced with mischief, and I could see immediately where Becca got her beguiling features. She was one of those people who exude an inner light—a people magnet, not the quiet, don't-look-at-me sort I ranked myself among.

"Where is she, by the way?" I looked around, expecting to find a caretaker or even Becca nearby. "Did you wheel yourself out here, Lily?"

"There you go again—stop worrying about me! Rebecca's taking a much-needed nap. She was up half the night fussing over me. I'm stronger than I look. Well, most of the time. One of my ever-present caretakers brought me out fifteen minutes ago, but I told him I wanted some time alone. Not much of it left to me, I'm afraid. Let's not talk of depressing things. We have an awful lot of catching up to do. Your Aunt Jessica filled you in on the story about Becca's birth, I'm told. And your grandmother Dorothea. And me?"

"Yes." I waited for her to go on.

She leveled her gaze at the water's looking-glass surface and spoke at length. "They say everyone should have the chance at a do-over. If I had mine, I would turn back the clock thirty-three years to when Rebecca was born. You never saw such a beautiful baby. She was a heartbreaker the minute she came out. But so was I back then—and I prided myself on it. If you can believe it, I was actually jealous of this baby whom I knew everyone would coo over. But it ran deeper than that. I also knew Rebecca would tie me to that dreadful cottage forever and become my ball and chain. Dorothea had cooped me up for so long I was ready to knock down the walls in my escape, if that's what it took. The boy I was dating said he would marry me after he learned I was pregnant. But with all my carelessness and pent-up passion for freedom, I knew I couldn't do *that*. So I ran away with him instead and left my baby at home, sure Dorothea would take care of her."

Lily took a tissue out of her pocket and coughed into it. "I never imagined she would give my baby away, but years later when I found out Rebecca was being raised as your sister, it all made perfect sense and I knew Dorothea had done the right thing."

I studied her face. "Didn't you ever miss her?"

She winced almost imperceptibly, and immediately I regretted my words. "I'm sorry—"

"No, it's all right. Terminal illness is a great leveler. If I can't be honest now, what's the point of going on at all? It's a fair question, Claire, and the answer is . . . yes and no. I was not my rightful self back then. And when I discovered I could numb all the pain of my wasted life with alcohol, I grew even more callous—and careless. It wasn't until my early forties that I started the slow journey back to my true self and felt the full weight of that decision made when I was sixteen. Oh, believe me, regret is a horrible thing. But by then I knew it would only confuse and wound Rebecca if I made a sudden reappearance in her life, stepping forward to reclaim her as my daughter. So I made the choice to keep silent and keep my distance, even though I was the one who now longed for relationship."

"But she knew," I said. "Did she tell you that? Becca somehow *knew* she was different, as she called it. Instinctively, I think she realized she didn't really belong to my mother—though she always belonged to me, in a manner of speaking."

Lily's face flushed with pleasure. "Yes, that she did. In fact, she's told me all about it—the stories of when you were little girls and you were her 'big skizzer.' When I left her in her bassinet that cold Saturday morning, I never dreamed I was pushing her toward a whole new destiny, but it seems that's what happened. She found herself in the sweetest sisterhood, and for that I will always be grateful. God knew just what my little Rebecca needed to make it in this world."

Lily reached out and squeezed my hand. "Thank you, Claire. You were part mother to her too, you know, not just a sister."

I gazed unblinking into her amber eyes. "I suppose I was. Yes—I think so."

The minutes seemed suspended until I glanced at my watch and realized we'd been talking for nearly an hour. Lily coughed again and said perhaps it was time to go in. I started to wheel her back to the monastery, but as if on cue Phineas Culver rounded the nearest outbuilding. "Let me do that, please." He looked at me sternly, his eyes large through the thick lenses of his glasses. "So I see you two have gotten acquainted."

Lily laughed like a girl. "Yes, Phinny, and don't you go scolding me or Claire for it either. It was the best gift I could have asked for today." She winked at me. "Phinny likes to scare people, but he knows by now I can see right through him. Inside he's a lump of sugar."

"You mean *he's* your caretaker?" I gasped. "Sorry—that came out wrong. It's just I had no idea."

The Englishman muttered something, and Lily laughed again. Phineas Culver's mouth twitched in an effort not to smile. He saved face by launching a query at me.

"So what's to become of our man in the moon, Ms.

Trowling? Does your sister know I've made a standing offer to purchase it? It's not too late to reconsider, you know."

"It's not mine to sell."

Lily watched the interplay between Phineas and me for a moment, a puzzled frown on her countenance. "Do you mean the family heirloom, Phinny, that old crescent moon pendant?"

"Yes, that's the one."

Her eyes snapped fire and she stopped the wheelchair abruptly, her blue-veined hands gripping the metal arms like a vise. "How dare you try to buy a treasure away from my daughter! I never heard a word about this." She whirled the chair around to face him, knocking Phineas in the knees as she did.

"My goodness! I didn't mean any harm—just a fair-value offer for a piece of jewelry that belongs back in Kellerby, its rightful place."

Lily eyed the little man with a steely gaze. "Don't you patronize me. I'm not dead yet, and I still know how to stand up and fight for what's dear to me."

He glanced down at her obvious sitting position, about to make an ironic remark, I supposed, but she cut him off in measured tones: "The pendant belongs to my daughter, Rebecca. There's more sentimental value wrapped up in that piece of gold than you'll ever fathom with your jeweler's loupe and cold heart."

And a minute ago he was a lump of sugar inside, I mused.

Phineas pushed his wire-rim glasses up the bridge of his nose and swept me a formal bow. "She's all yours, Ms. Trowling. I wash my hands of her—and bid you good day. When you two are finished with your little tête-à-tête, you can wheel her into the dining hall and have the monk on duty ring for me."

"I can wheel myself back! I told you I'm not dead yet!" she called after his retreating figure, the effort of her rage leaving her trembling. "I'm not dead yet," she repeated, barely audible. A tear spilled over and trickled down her cheek, and I stood there awkwardly, shell-shocked at the strength of her fury and the uncomfortable scene I had just witnessed.

Lily sobbed softly in her wheelchair, the same sound that had drawn me into the garden to find her an hour ago. I knelt and wrapped my arms around her shoulders.

"Hey, now, don't let that creepy little man work you into a fever. He's not worth it."

She nuzzled her head against my arm and sniffed. "He's really not all that bad—just brought the mother bear out in me. After willfully giving Rebecca away all those years ago, that pendant was like the gift of my heart back to her from afar. It contains a part of me."

Her words hovered in the air, and I sat back on the carpet of grass, running over them again in my mind.

She saw my bewilderment, or perhaps it was the look of dawning revelation on my face. "What is it, Claire? Have I said something to disturb you?"

"So it was you. And all this time I thought . . ."

"Yes, go on." She had the expectant look of one awaiting a verdict. "What was it you thought, Claire?"

"Well, that Dorothea had gifted Becca with the crescent moon pendant. She showed it to me one day not long after we found the cottage in the woods, and I just always thought . . ."

Lily leaned forward in the wheelchair. "That it was a grandmother's gift to one particular granddaughter—leaving the other out?"

"After seeing the special bond between Dorothea and Becca when we were girls, why, I just naturally assumed . . ."

"Listen to me, Claire. I was given that pendant on my sixteenth birthday—Dorothea said she wanted me to have it. I suppose in her canny way she knew I wouldn't be around much longer. When I left home for good a few months later, I left behind two things—my baby daughter and the crescent moon pendant, with a part of myself inside and a note to pass it to Rebecca when she was old enough to take care of it."

"A part of yourself . . . I don't understand."

She smiled, and the pale sunlight filtering through the trees reflected in her amber eyes. "Did you never realize the pendant is actually a locket?"

I shook my head, mute.

"I snipped off a tiny lock of my hair and placed it inside the pendant. There's a hidden catch in the back; not everyone sees it at first."

Now I was the one whose eyes welled with tears. I

blinked them back and returned her smile. "I hope Becca realizes the real treasure is you, Lily. She's found you so late in life, but what a remarkable discovery you are."

I stood to my feet and wheeled her back to the dining room, where she insisted I leave her for now. As I turned to go, one lingering question came to mind.

"Lily, the music box that was delivered to our house one Christmas when Becca and I were girls—was that you too?"

She pressed her finger to her lips, her eyes sparkling with mischief. "Shhh. It's our secret."

The monk with dining hall duty that day bustled forward to wheel Lily back to her quarters. I watched until they turned the corner down a long connecting corridor, the wheelchair's rhythmic squeaking echoing fainter and fainter as they were swallowed up by the monastery's vastness.

24

Kellerby, England
June 2001

Colin moved about the Rectory grounds with his nonchalant grace, supervising the event setup, which seemed to grow more complex by the hour. Saturday afternoon the mayor phoned to say a celebrated string quartet was driving all the way from Manchester to take part in the event.

Toward dusk on Saturday evening I found Colin in the glade of the walled garden, clipping fresh flowers for the party tables and making gladiolus garlands for the church pews. He looked up as I parted the willow tree curtain to join him and sat cross-legged on the grass.

"Ah, my partner in crime. I could use some help about now, Claire."

I shot a glance at his face to read any double meaning that might be there, hoping for one. "If I were you I'd be completely frazzled by now. How do you keep so cool under pressure, Colin?"

He laughed as he twined two gladiolus with string and then held out two more for me to bind. "Call it the gift of the magi, if you like. My mother always told me I was very much like my father that way—quiet, easy-going. I suppose everybody has to have at least one good trait."

I swatted him playfully with a bit of twine. "Oh, I can think of a few more than just that one—and now we can add 'humble' to the list too."

His face grew serious, and he looked down to select two more flowers. "I never even met him."

"Your father, you mean?"

"Yes." Several minutes passed in silence before he spoke again. "It's why I've always backed away from the idea of getting married. I knew that if I did, I would wind up having children like every good Englishman does. But then what? Would I abandon my wife and kids too? Who's to say a trait like that isn't carried through the blood? Who's to say I would be more of a man than he was? To be honest, the fear of failure keeps me away."

The raw vulnerability of his words stunned me, and I did a very bold thing—for me. I reached over, took his hand in mine, and squeezed it until he met my eyes. I saw tears shimmering in them, lighted by the rising moon. I chose my words carefully, knowing full well that moments like this don't drop into one's lap every day—certainly not mine.

"Colin, you're the kindest man I've ever known. It's true I haven't dated a lot, but I have had enough experience to know a good man when I see one. You're a keeper, Colin—the very best kind of man. And you would never abandon your wife and children. I think the woman who finds favor in your eyes will be the luckiest woman on earth."

His eyes flickered, and my heart lurched in my chest. I had said too much. Now it was my turn to glance down, afraid he would see the hot flush in my cheeks even in the twilight.

To my horror he actually laughed, but it was a kind-hearted chuckle, not a laugh of derision. "Claire, you always manage to say the most amazing things. And you even tolerate my silences without any awkwardness." He dropped my hand, and we fell into one of those long silences again, twining flowers two by two. After a few minutes he looked up at me. "Thank you" was all he said.

We wove more garlands together, passing the time in easy conversation. The moon rose high and white, making a pool of light in the garden glade where we worked. Eventually Colin lit a few lanterns, and I asked him the question that had been on my mind for the past few days—stirred up by all the talk of blessings and baptisms, requiem and regret, God and . . . I didn't know what.

"Colin, twenty years ago you told me a story about what happened to you one night when you wandered into the chapel on your college campus."

He nodded, smiling. "Yes, the night I heard the sexton singing. Amazing."

"Is that the night God became real for you? Because if so, I need a dose of the same medicine." He waited for me to go on. "I grew up thinking I knew God—or at least knew about him. But over a lifetime of disappointments you can get pretty jaded on the whole religion thing, you know? It's been a long time since I even tried."

Colin stood to his feet, grabbing the bundle of garlands in one hand and reaching the other out to me. "Well, perhaps that's your problem, love. When was the last time you *tried* to catch a moonbeam on your shoulder? You probably weren't successful. Yet just now, when you weren't even aware of it, I saw a shaft of moonlight illuminate you in the most beautiful way."

I took his hand and followed him to the storage shed, where we piled the garlands onto a worktable and put the newly clipped flowers into jugs of water for tomorrow. As we turned to leave the shed, Colin fixed me with that gentle gaze of his and said words I would never forget. "I read something in a book several years ago that I'm going to share with you now. This American monk wrote, 'Let there always be quiet, dark churches in which people can take refuge . . . houses of God filled with his silent presence. There, even when they do not know how to pray, at least they can be still and breathe easily.'"

He looked at me steadily. "Breathe easily, Claire. If your heart is as open as it sounds, God will fall all over himself to rush out to meet you."

I wanted to tell him that indeed my heart was opening—to God, to the prospect of loving again—and that he was the catalyst for both. In time I knew I would tell him. But for now, instead, I gave voice to the complex emotions that had been swirling inside me for the past week—thoughts about my sister Becca, the curious love-hate relationship I'd had with her over the years, the way I both adored and resented her, often at the same time. What do you do with feelings like that, I asked him. He was wise enough not to answer, knowing the question was rhetorical.

We parted at the inn's stairway that night, me to climb up to the master suite and fall into an exhausted sleep, he to do one or two more tasks before the night ended. The door to Rainey's alcove was shut, and I felt relieved. I wasn't in the mood to talk to anyone else.

After washing up, I slipped into my long white nightgown and sat in the window seat of the arched window, staring up at the moon. Years ago Colin had told me the right melody is like a prayer. I remembered a lullaby Mama sang to Becca and me as little girls and started humming. On a night just like this, with the moon blinding bright, she called us out to the back porch of our old house and patted the porch swing. That was all the cue we needed. Clambering up beside her, giddy and giggling, we lay against her breast, our own arms entwined, and listened as she sang a lullaby and rocked us in the moonlight. In that memory, at least, I saw us as a happy trio, with no one left out.

Once again I felt the need to pray, but all I could muster was Mama's lullaby—my song-prayer to God that everything would come out right in the end. And this time I was sure God heard it. The sound of feet crunching along the gravel drive two stories below broke my reverie, and I glanced to see who it was. There was Colin, his flute bag flung over his shoulder as he headed for the dirt road that led to the church, most likely to make his own song-prayer on the eve of the reconsecration ceremony. I imagined him climbing up to the bell tower—the place where all the horror began four centuries ago—and bending his head over the flute to create a melody so sublime the angels would pause to listen. Just before he disappeared from view, he turned and lifted his hand in a silent salute to me. I waved back, wondering if he'd felt me watching him.

The sound of drizzling rain woke me early Sunday morning. I crawled out of bed and pulled the curtain back to assess the gray morning. Wet or not, this day had a lot riding on it. I hoped for Father Bernard's sake that a small crowd would still gather at St. Barnabas for the ceremony, four hours from now. I showered and went downstairs for breakfast, then caught up with Colin in the back hallway as he headed out to the shed.

His smile lit up his handsome features. "Ah, there you are, Claire. Are you looking for a chore to pass the time, because if so I could use your help tying the garlands onto the church pews."

"Sure, anything. Where's Rainey?"

"Your brother-in-law is pacing in the garden. I wouldn't disturb him just now if I were you. He looks deep in thought—and a bit agitated. I suppose we can't blame him for that."

Colin was right. I knew Rainey must be wrestling with his own whirlwind of emotions right now, aware that he would be reunited with Becca in a few hours.

We avoided the part of the garden that would take us past Rainey and circled to the shed from the other way around. Stacking the garlands in the back of Colin's pickup, we drove to the church because of the drizzle and started dressing the pews fit for a wedding. An hour flew by and then another. Father Bernard had brought over from the monastery a brass plate and cup for the sacraments, as well as a large brass cross for the altar. Colin and I polished the brass until we could see our faces in it, laughing as we told each other stories from our childhood.

Sometime during the church-dressing the rain stopped, and thin, watery sunshine filtered through the cloud cover. I only became aware of it when Colin stopped his story abruptly and nodded at something over my shoulder, his face glowing from the colorful light streaming through a stained-glass window.

"I'll go for now," he said. "Someone wants to see you."

Before I could answer he ducked through a side exit and was gone. I turned to see my sister standing in the church's arched doorway, a dark silhouette with a tangle of golden curls. She stepped forward into St. Barnabas's gloomy interior, and my eyes adjusted to the familiar sight of Becca, her mouth curved into that pixie smile that made men love her and women wish they'd been born with better features.

I opened my mouth to speak, but she got there first. "Oh, Claire! It's just like when we were girls, remember? Except that creepy old devil face doesn't have the power to scare us anymore." She spread her arms wide and twirled slowly, her eyes closed, as if breathing in the history of the place. When she stopped and opened her eyes she laughed, closing the space between us quickly to crush me in a bear hug. "I came over early from the monastery to see the place alone and relive our memories. And instead I found you."

After a few seconds I pulled away to look into her eyes. "Becca, why didn't you tell us? We could have worked it out somehow. Do you know how frantic you've made Rainey? Why all this drama?"

She shook her head, her eyes pooling fast. "It's okay, Claire. Everything's going to be all right, you'll see. I love Rainey—I love you—but . . . You know why I had to go away, don't you? Father Bernard told me you did. You of all people should know, after the way we lost Mama without a chance to say good-bye. When I realized there was someone in the world who gave me life—my own true mother—I couldn't let her die without getting to know her first. It's funny, I always felt like a misfit in our family, but I never knew why. Now I do. These past two weeks with Lily have been worth it, Claire, no matter what you and Rainey say."

We settled in a pew near the altar and leaned our arms on the pew-back in front of us. Outside I could hear the men setting up the tents and long tables for the after-party. Somebody turned on a portable radio, blaring rock music.

"I saw our grandmother again," I said. "Rainey and I visited her at the cottage. Funny calling her that, when all she ever was to me was Gretchen, the strange old lady in the woods."

"So I heard. How'd it go? I hope she didn't freak you out too much." Becca studied me as she spoke; I wondered if the subtle change I'd undergone in the past week showed on the outside.

I rested my chin on my forearm and smiled. "Well, there's no getting around her eccentricity, that's for sure. But she's . . . endearing . . . in a way. I hope we have a chance to get better acquainted sometime."

"Oh, I think you will. In fact, she and Aunt Jess will be here today."

I looked at her in surprise. "You're kidding me. Why didn't anyone say something? You mean Dorothea and Aunt Jess came all the way to England for the ceremony today?"

"Mmm-hmm." She nodded, her head jostling as it rested on her own forearm. "Lily touched base with both of them by phone this week. I wanted it to be a surprise." Becca grinned, awaiting my response.

"Well . . . miracles never cease, do they? I bet Aunt Jess will bellow for someone to carry her luggage again. Do you remember that? And the way she stalked into the Rectory like she owned the place?" We burst into laughter, recalling our imperious aunt stumping her way through England, us hapless girls in tow.

We grew quiet for a few minutes, and after a while I said the words that were on both our minds. "Becca, about you and me . . . everything Aunt Jess told me this week kind of threw me for a loop."

She gazed at me steadily, her amber eyes full of compassion. "It's all right, Claire. I've had a little longer to get used to the idea. Dorothea first told me in a letter about six months ago. That's also when she finally told me she was my—our—grandmother, but I think inside I already knew we were connected somehow. By blood, I mean."

"It doesn't make you feel . . . I don't know . . . distant from me somehow?" I hoped my words didn't sound cold.

Becca sat upright, her face almost stern. "Not at all. Like I said, I've had longer to get used to the idea, but the way I see it, Claire, nothing between us need change. Nothing *is* changed except a birth record somewhere in North Carolina."

She told me about Lily, the mother she'd never known, and what the past few weeks with her had been like. Becca described a woman with a firebrand nature tempered by time and hard experience, then mellowed into sweetness by God. She talked about their walks around the monastery grounds, Becca pushing the wheelchair slowly. I could picture her gazing at Lily's face as if trying to read her own life story there.

"No, it was the right thing to slip away as I did," Becca said finally, "even though it must have hurt Rainey terribly. You know how he is, Claire. He never would have let me go off alone for so long—he's so overprotective."

"Am I?" a deep voice echoed in the nave, and both Becca and I turned to see Rainey stepping into the church from outside.

"Sweetheart!" she called.

"It's only because I love you so much," he said, never breaking stride as he made his way down the long aisle toward her, burying his face in her hair. "Oh, it's good to see you, Becca. Please don't ever scare me like that again."

And then it was my turn to make my exit through a side doorway, allowing husband and wife time alone in the garlanded church to get reacquainted. Outside in the churchyard I found Colin grinning like a Cheshire cat as he closed the bed of his pickup. He looked up at the bell tower and then let his eyes sweep over the grounds of St. Barnabas.

"This old place will taste the resurrection and the life today, Claire, and you play a big part in that."

"Me?" I looked at him quizzically. "What did—"

"Shhh." He cut me off gently, placing his finger on my lips, his eyes crinkled in a smile. "Don't spoil the moment, love, just bask in it. And look—it seems we're in for quite a party after all."

I followed his gaze up the dirt road and saw a long string of cars winding their way toward the stone church. In spite of the day's rainy start, Kellerby had come out en masse to celebrate a new beginning.

25

Kellerby, England
June 2001

Half an hour later, squeezed into the front pew of St. Barnabas, we listened as Father Bernard performed the service of reconsecration. The old monk beamed out at the congregation as he singsonged the words that brought down God's blessing on the stone church.

"Everliving Father, watchful and caring, our source and our end: all that we are and all that we have is yours. Accept us now, as we dedicate this place to which we come to praise your Name . . ."

I peeked around and saw every pew in the church filled to capacity. Quite a few people had even squeezed into the choir loft that formed a small balcony to the left of the altar. Some of the faces looked familiar to me after my weeklong visit to Kellerby. There was Janey Smithton, beaming beneath her broad-brimmed Sunday hat. I scanned the rows. Toward the front across the aisle I spotted Father Desmond, from the church in downtown Kellerby, who caught my eye and winked. Sitting next to him was the mayor—almost difficult to recognize with dry hair and clothes, since the last time I'd seen him he was soaked from the dunking cage.

". . . Lord Jesus Christ, make this a temple of your presence and a house of prayer. Be always near us when we seek you in this place. Draw us to you, when we come alone and when we come with others, to find comfort and wisdom, to be supported and strengthened, to rejoice and give thanks. May it be here, Lord Christ, that we are made one with you and with one another, so that our lives are sustained and sanctified for your service."

A door in the back creaked open, and the congregation craned their necks to see two elderly women, most definitely Americans, step inside the nave. One of them was tall and moved with a dancer's grace even at her age. Her iron-gray hair was pulled into a neat chignon at the nape of her neck, and her vintage black clothing and veiled hat vaguely reminded me of the outfit she'd worn to see Becca's performance at the Thanksgiving play years ago. The other woman, though slightly hunched with age, led the two and moved with a benighted force that spoke of vigor and a domineering personality. Her close-cropped silver hair matched a shimmering brooch on her suit lapel. I nudged Becca as we watched Aunt Jess and Dorothea take the seats reserved for them.

"The peace of the Lord be with you!" Father Bernard called out.

"And also with you," we answered back.

"Let us give thanks to the Lord our God."

"It is right to give him thanks and praise."

Crammed together as we were, it was hard not to be distracted by Aunt Jess and Dorothea settling in their seats, but Father Bernard cleared his throat loudly. "Six hundred years ago the citizens of Kellerby came together to build, stone by stone, this magnificent house of God." Father Bernard clasped his wrinkled hands beneath the long cross that hung around his neck and leaned toward his congregation. "Every Sunday for two centuries the bells of St. Barnabas rang out, and the faithful gathered here to worship God. Until something dark happened, and we foolishly allowed the darkness to chase the light away. Let us remember the faithful words of Christ: 'You are the light of the world. A city that is set on a hill cannot be hidden. Nor do they light a lamp and put it under a basket, but on a lampstand, and it gives light to all who are in the house. Let your light so shine before men that they may see your good works and glorify your Father in heaven.' Let us never hide our light, and the light of St. Barnabas, again . . ."

After his sermon Father Bernard asked Becca and Lily to step forward, and he performed a ritual of blessing on mother and daughter, anointing their foreheads with oil as he intoned the words of Christ. I saw him lightly touch the gold crescent moon pendant around Becca's neck as he prayed. Becca's eyes were pooling fast; Lily gazed back at her daughter with what struck me as stoic grace. I could picture her minuscule lock of hair inside the pendant around Becca's neck. *A part of myself . . .* When the ritual ended and the celebration of the Eucharist began, Becca reclaimed her place by my side, slipped the pendant around my neck, and then clasped my hand.

"It rightfully belongs to you, Claire," she whispered. "You're the eldest sister in the family. And besides, you're the most likely one to have children someday. Someone's got to pass it on."

I looked at her startled and saw her nod ever so slightly toward Colin standing on my right. "The power of Christ compels you," she intoned as if she were Father Bernard.

I almost laughed out loud. The old monk gestured to the congregation, and we rose for the final benediction. The organist leaned on the keys of the pipe organ, and the sudden surge of music swelled to the rafters of the ancient church. As we all stood to our feet and sang the words of Martin Luther's famous hymn, Colin took my other hand and squeezed it tight. I glanced up and met his eyes. Even without a word being spoken, I knew a silent understanding passed between us.

Father Desmond stepped to the altar as the congregation started to break up and lifted his hands like a teacher trying to regain control of a noisy class. "Thank you, thank you for coming here today, every one of you. Wasn't it good to hear our beloved Father Bernard preach a sermon again after so long?"

The crowd murmured and then broke into spontaneous applause for the elderly monk, who looked abashed at the sudden attention. Phineas Culver stood awkwardly at his side blinking out at the crowd like an owl, as if stupefied they had all showed up.

Father Desmond went on. "The best part is yet to come. We invite you to stay on the grounds for the St. Barnabas Reconsecration Ceremony After Party. It'll be a gathering fit for a king. You don't want to miss it!"

During the hour-long ceremony inside the stone church, Colin's volunteer staff had transformed the grounds of St. Barnabas and the Rectory into something out of a medieval fair. Tables and chairs dotted the grounds with festive banners flapping in the breeze. Someone had erected a Maypole that stood forlorn, but I imagined it encircled by excited children later in the day. The string quartet from Manchester was tuning its instruments on a makeshift stage area Colin had built beneath a shade tree. A drama troupe, costumed from the medieval era, laid out a huge checkered cloth and staked it to the ground. After studying their costumes I realized they were preparing for a "human chess match" that would come to life that afternoon. Under the main tent, Tilda oversaw the unloading of steaming trays of food brought down from the Rectory, and various others from Kellerby's fund-raising groups assembled side dishes, drinks, and desserts to round out the fare.

I caught up with Becca, her arm twined around Rainey's waist and a soft, contented look in her eyes.

Instinctively I touched the pendant around my neck. "It's good to see you two together again. Rainey, if you clutch her any harder she'll break."

My brother-in-law threw his head back and laughed. "Believe me, she's not leaving my side all day."

"And who says I want to?" Becca teased, smiling up at her husband. "Claire, did you know about all this hoopla? I thought it was just going to be a ceremony, not a . . . county fair!"

"So you got more than you bargained for," Colin said, striding by with an armful of folding chairs. "If you stick around long enough there'll be fireworks tonight."

"Ooh, did I hear somebody say fireworks?" We turned to see Lily approaching on foot, leaning on a cane as she came up the cobblestone path that led from the church's main door. It was good to see her upright. She scanned our faces and smiled. "Well, I believe there's enough fanfare right here to rival any fireworks! Rainey, we haven't properly met. I'm—"

"My mother," Becca jumped in, tucking a long spiral curl behind her ear. "And it's about time you two finally met. Oh, Rainey, we have so much to tell you, darling. These past few weeks with Lily have been among the most wonderful of my life."

She and Lily chatted on about how they had filled their days and nights at the monastery guesthouse, reading books aloud to each other, helping Father Bernard with his note-taking, wandering the grounds, counting stars in the night sky as they lay like disobedient children, way past their bedtime, on the floor of the Juliet balcony that adjoined their room, telling stories from the missing years—the years Becca was desperately trying to make up for in these final days of Lily's life. How much time did she have left? It was the unspoken question in all our minds. Scanning their faces, I was reminded of mirror images in a funhouse—the same perfect female features, haloed by golden blonde curls, but one countenance changed slightly by time and illness. I felt an odd twinge of jealousy over their mother-daughter bond, knowing it was something I would never share in.

"Here come the dowagers," Rainey muttered, looking over our heads in the direction of the church. "Everyone, gird your loins."

Becca nudged him playfully in the ribs with her elbow. "Grandmother, Aunt Jess, over here! Come say hello to everybody. It's so wonderful to see you both again. How was your trip across the Atlantic?"

Lily and I exchanged glances and almost giggled like schoolgirls.

"Well, we made it in one piece, didn't we?" Aunt Jess said flatly. "I see the whole lot of you have gathered here for this shindig. Lucky for you I was able to drag Dorothea out from that horrible cottage of hers."

"And the effort was worth it, my dears. Despite what your grumpy old aunt says." Dorothea settled her eyes on Becca and me as she linked her arm through Lily's protectively. "Even that turbulent stretch across the Atlantic. My word, I never thought I'd see the inside of a train again, let alone an airplane. Not my mode of travel, I can tell you. Perhaps I'll persuade Jessica to book passage on a ship for the return trip home."

Becca almost snorted. "This isn't the 1930s, Grandmother. It would take you days to get home."

"I wish Eugenia Lockwood was here for our little party," Aunt Jess said suddenly. "We had the loveliest visit here twenty years ago, didn't we, girls? Claire, where has Mr. Lockwood taken himself off to? I thought I saw him walk by here just a few minutes ago. Carrying chairs like a hired man, for crying out loud. Is he doing well? I can't help but think he must be struggling terribly now that the Rectory is his responsibility. Eugenia had such a gift for running an inn. Hardly something a gardener would be good at—"

"I don't know, Aunt Jess, why don't you ask him yourself? Here he comes right now." I looked up to greet Colin as he approached in those long, easy strides of his, arms empty of their burden now. "Colin, my aunt Jess has a question for you."

"Sure, fire away." He joined our small cluster, resting his hands on his hips and waiting politely for my elderly aunt to speak.

Aunt Jess looked flustered and waved her hand dismissively. "It's nothing. Another time, perhaps." She fixed me with a chilly glare. I smiled, triumphant, as I locked gazes with her. Out the corner of my eye I saw Becca and Rainey stifle laughter.

"Well, then, here's the thing, I came to let you all know

the food is ready. Tilda has outdone herself as usual. Why don't you let me help you to that stand of trees over there? I've just set up a table and chairs for my favorite guests." Colin extended his arm in the old-fashioned way, and Dorothea took it, seeing Aunt Jess hesitate.

I never imagined we band of Americans, surrounded by a crowd of festivity-seeking English citizens, would be so popular, but it was true. As the afternoon wore on I lost count of the number of people who joined our circle for a chat, or asked us to take part in some game that was about to begin on the far side of the grounds. Even the children seemed fascinated by our funny American accents, giggling shyly as they asked us to say words like *library* and *advertisement* again and again.

Near the dinner hour, Father Desmond, who had assumed the role of master of ceremonies, stood up on the musicians' stage and spoke through the microphone. "Testing, one-two. Testing. Can everyone hear me?" He tapped the microphone with his forefinger, and we winced as an ear-splitting sound of feedback blared through the speakers. "Sorry about that. Just wanted to know you were all still awake," he deadpanned, sliding into his role of emcee with ease. A murmur of laughter rippled through the crowd. "Some of you have other obligations for the evening, and we understand if you have to go. You will be missed! But for those of you who still have a bit of juice in your batteries, stick around for the evening's festivities—or take a break at home and then return later tonight. There'll be dancing under the stars over there"—we all turned to look in the direction he pointed to a section of the grounds marked off by colorful lanterns strung up to light the evening—"and, to cap off this historic day's events, a solemn bagpipe procession from the Rectory to the bell tower of St. Barnabas. This is a day the town of Kellerby will never forget, and we want every one of you to be a part of it."

Some of the crowd broke up after Father Desmond's speech, wandering off toward their cars parked up the dirt road by the Rectory. I watched them go, mildly disappointed, wanting the festive spirit to maintain its momentum. I must have sighed audibly, for Colin suddenly said, "Don't worry, most of them will be back. It is going to be a rather long day. Are you sure you don't want to rest for a while? I can promise you I'll get your blood surging again later this evening."

I looked at him, shocked and delighted at his bold words.

"I meant by dancing," he laughed. "You should see your face right now, Claire. But you will let me partner you in a dance or two, won't you? I've been looking forward to that all day."

I had forgotten how long the days stretch on in the English summertime. Well into the evening hours the pale sunlight shone down on us, sunset seeming like an elusive far-off event. Already worn out from the full day, I took Colin's suggestion and napped in my room at the Rectory while the "dowagers" returned to their hotel in town. Phineas Culver drove Lily back to the monastery, and Becca and Rainey wandered off to be alone together. We all promised to meet up again later that night.

A light tap on my door woke me from a fitful sleep. I glanced at the bedside clock and realized it was almost 10:00 p.m. "Evening, miss," a voice called from the hallway. It was the young woman who ran the front desk. "Colin said not to let you sleep too long or you'll miss the best part of the evening."

"Right, yes . . . tell him I'll be down in just a second." Still groggy with sleep, I splashed cool water on my face and slipped into some clean clothes, then retouched my face. When I came downstairs fifteen minutes later, the Rectory lobby was empty. So were the parlor, the dining room, the kitchen, and the back hallway. Through the old Tudor's open windows I heard lively music drifting up the dirt road from the grounds of St. Barnabas. Someone sawed an Irish jig on a fiddle, and I could picture couples swinging round and round on the makeshift dance floor.

Hurrying out through the walled garden, I crested the small hill of the dirt road, remembering again the first time I set foot on this very same English soil twenty years ago. Where was Colin? Under the lantern lights I could see a crowd clustered on the party grounds, two dozen couples or more dancing and the first stars peeping out of the sky.

"Why, there you are!" Father Desmond rushed up from a small group of people standing near the musicians' stage and pumped my hand. "I missed you earlier today in all the merry madness, but it's so good to see you again, Ms. Trowling. Did those vegetables from the market work out to your liking? Trust you're having a good time?"

"Absolutely," I said, answering both queries at once. "You weren't kidding about a party fit for a king. How long's the dancing been going on? I think I slept half the night away just now."

"Not to worry. They just started up an hour ago. By the way, someone is looking for you—your dance partner, perhaps?" The Anglican priest's eyes crinkled in a smile, and as a parishioner pulled his attention away I turned to scan the crowd in the lantern light.

The music stopped, the laughing couples clinging to each other as they regrouped for the next song. They didn't have to wait long. A beautiful haunting melody drifted out over the night as the musicians slowed things down, drawing even more couples onto the floor for a slow dance. Swallowing my frustration, I wandered down the cobblestone path that led to the church and then veered into the graveyard, the stones turning silvery white in the starlight.

"You promised me a dance," a voice spoke out of the velvety darkness. I turned and there was Colin, his lean frame propped against the door of the ancient stone church. In the twilight I couldn't make out his expression, but I heard the tone in his voice.

"Father Desmond said you were looking for me," I began.

"And here you are." He walked up to me and extended his hand in a formal gesture. Without a word he led me in a slow dance there among the gravestones, the musicians' melody carrying down to us on the night breeze. "Your sister and brother-in-law are staying on at the Rectory for another week, Claire. I thought perhaps you might too." He gazed down at me. "Now that you're back, you know, I can't let you slip away again so easily."

I started to make some sort of teasing reply, but a faint sound from up the road stopped us both where we stood on the spongy grass.

"Shhh, listen," he said, though I'd not uttered a word. The music had vanished and in its place we heard the mournful strains of a bagpipe. "It's the procession Father Desmond spoke of. Let's join them."

Linking my arm through his, Colin led the way in the darkness toward the procession of people descending the hill, and with them we backtracked to the foot of St. Barnabas. As the piper leaned into his instrument, creating a melody so somber it almost split our souls, I looked up at the gray stone church before me. So much in my life had started in this place, and now it seemed God was bringing it all full circle.

Leading the procession, the old monk carried the cross of Christ, its gleaming brass catching flickers of light from the distant lanterns and the flashlights among the crowd. As he said a prayer over St. Barnabas—and the people who would *be* the church there—it occurred to me that God had answered my prayer after all. Things had come out right in the end.

The old priest prayed on, and I saw a teenage boy slip up to the bell tower as if on cue. Suddenly Father Bernard lifted his head, his eyes shining with youthful vigor. "The bell of St. Barnabas has not rung out over these hills for nigh on forty years, my friends. It's high time she rang out again—tonight!"

Standing so near to the bell tower, I felt a tremor in my chest as the enormous bell *clong, clong, clonged* into the night sky and a roaring cheer rose up from the crowd. Our breath suspended, heads tilted back, we stood stock-still as the boy swung up and down on the massive rope, ringing the bell again and again.

Without thinking, my hand went to my throat, and I felt the crescent moon pendant there. The locket with Lily's tiny curl of hair in it. The heirloom gift from my sister. In that instant Colin reached both arms around me, and I had the sudden sense of coming home.

Acknowledgments

Thank you, Janet Kobobel Grant, for believing in the story of *Skizzer*—and for taking a chance on me as a first-time novelist.

A special thanks goes to the team at Revell for their passion and professionalism in bringing this book to market: Lonnie Hull DuPont, Kristin Kornoelje, Cat Hoort, Erin Bartels, Brooke Nolen, Claudia Marsh, Cheryl Van Andel, and Dave Lewis and his amazing sales team.

To the special people who "held my hand" throughout the long journey of *Skizzer*, including Jeanette Thomason, Debbie Cole, Marcia Ford, Janet Angelo, Melissa Bogdany, David Ross, Paige Lehnert, my daughters Kate and Emily, and my online writing group friends Margaret Feinberg, Lori Smith, and Michael D. Warden.

Finally, I would like to thank the proprietor of the real-world Rectory Inn whose name I don't even recall (from 1997), but whose lovely bed and breakfast near Thirsk, England—complete with a fascinating stone church just beyond—inspired the setting for the parts of this story that take place in England.

A. J. Kiesling is a former religion writer for *Publishers Weekly* and the author of several books, including *Jaded: Hope for Believers Who Have Given Up on Church but Not on God* (Baker). This is her first novel. She can be reached by email at wordsmith351@yahoo.com, or via her website at ajkiesling.com.